Secrets of the

TREE HOUSE

ENJOY!

LEINAD

Secrets of the

TREE HOUSE

The Tree House is a place where you are never...Alone!

LEINAD PLATZ

MILL CITY PRESS

Xulon Press
2301 Lucien Way #415
Maitland, FL 32751
407.339.4217
www.xulonpress.com

Paperback ISBN-13: 978-1-66284-114-9
Hard Cover ISBN-13: 978-1-66284-115-6
Ebook ISBN-13: 978-1-66284-116-3

DEDICATION

Secretes of the Tree House, is dedicated to
my loving and supportive wife.

Beth

Thank you for… *EVERYTHING!*

CHAPTER 1

I walked into the boy's restroom and saw Robert Schultz pinning my friend Jimmie Becker to the tile wall, a hand around Jimmie's throat.

"Hey!" I yelled, lurching forward to push Robert away.

Robert went tumbling onto the floor, his expression one of shocked anger. His face was bright red and confused.

I stood over him, my fists balled up. I glanced at Jimmie.

"You okay?"

"Yeah." He was gently rubbing his throat.

Robert scrambled back, trying to get to his feet. He was a worm, a prick, and now he looked like a frightened puppy. It would be easy to say that since he was a bully, Robert looked like a caveman...but in reality, he was one of the handsome guys.

Robert stood, wiping his palms on his jeans, eyeing me warily.

"Get out," I said.

And I didn't have to tell him twice. He was gone in a flash.

I looked at Jimmie. "What was that all about?"

He shrugged. "I guess I looked at him wrong."

"He do anything?"

Jimmie shrugged again. He's a good head shorter than me even though we'll both turn sixteen soon.

"Naw, just...you know..." *making fun of me* was probably the rest of that sentence. I'd seen it happen a couple of times in the locker room, and it ain't cool. But what could anyone do? Some guys hit puberty later than others.

"You need me to take care of him, I will," I said. Although Robert and I had similar builds, I suspected he could kick my ass if he wanted.

"I can handle myself."

I nodded, even though I didn't believe him.

And that's when the bell rang. Jimmie hurried off.

He might be my friend—maybe my only friend—but, he sure was skittish.

Jimmie and I shared homeroom, but we didn't talk.

After fourth period, I saw Robert coming down the hall in my direction. When he saw me, he did an about-face and left through the rear doors where he'd come in.

I smirked.

In the locker room after P.E., Jimmie finished tying his shoes while I pulled on a sock. "Meet at the Tree House?"

"Sure," Jimmie said. "Don't you have to work?"

"I don't know. I gotta ask Mr. Kraus if he needs me today or not."

He nodded, then stood and left.

Mr. Kraus wasn't home, and Emma, the Kraus's housekeeper, said he hadn't left any instructions for me. So, I got on my bike and headed home.

When I went up the driveway, past my dad's car, and came around the corner of the house into the backyard, I saw Jimmie's bike was leaning up against the tree. Up above, in the tree house, I could hear a hammering sound.

Thunk, thunk...thunk...thunk, thunk.

It was a warm day, and I wanted to go to my room and change into shorts, but I was more curious about what Jimmie was doing. I climbed up the boards on the trunk leading into the tree house.

Apparently, Jimmie didn't hear me.

"Hey!" I said as I popped up through the opening in the floor.

Jimmie spun around, surprised, holding a hammer. Then he scrambled, scooting himself across the floor, ending up against the far wall under the stained-glass window, his blue eyes wide. His curly blond hair looked more messy than usual, and he was breathing heavily.

He then hung his head and let out a long sigh, shaking his head.

"What's wrong?"

"I think I killed him," Jimmie said.

"Killed who? With what?"

Then he looked up and pointed to the bark of the tree where the end of a spent bullet casing jutted out. That was what he had been hammering.

I moved in closer and noticed its primer had been struck.

"That crusty old man who scares people off his property," Jimmie said.

Immediately, I knew who he meant.

"You...shot...Mr. Wendorf?"

Before he could answer, we heard, *"It's time for dinner!"* It was my mother yelling out the door.

Jimmie dropped the hammer onto the floor and slid past me without saying another word, disappearing through the floor, down the tree, onto his bike, and speeding into the woods.

Half of me didn't want to believe Jimmie. But he had seemed so scared. And the empty bullet casing...was he trying to hide it? Was Mr. Wendorf dead?

Then I heard my mom.

"It's time for dinner!"

The next morning, 7:05 am, I got on the school bus and purposely sat on the left side so that—at about a quarter mile down the road—I could see Mr. Wendorf's house. It was an old, weathered farmhouse, set back off the road, slightly hidden behind some tall oak and maple trees.

When we got there, I could see the tail end of Wendorf's pickup truck sticking out from behind his house. I recalled that normally, it was parked along the side with its grill facing the road.

Other than that, nothing looked out of place. Actually, pretty normal—a little broken down and somewhat eerie.

The next house on our route was Jimmie's, and the bus came to a stop. Jimmie got on and sat a couple rows up from me. He didn't always sit with me, depended on his mood. The other kids on the bus paid no attention to his arrival. They just continued jabbering or staring out the windows.

Did Jimmie really kill Mr. Wendorf? If so, why?

It was another day at school, like any other day. Nothing unusual. Jimmie kept to himself, though I did notice he went back for seconds at the lunch counter. That probably meant he'd had no breakfast.

After school, the bus came to a stop, dropping Jimmie off.

I slid over to switch seats so I could take another look at Mr. Wendorf's house before getting off the bus myself.

Nothing seemed different. Truck hadn't moved; everything looked the same.

My father had been the pastor at the Believers Fellowship Church since before I was born, so I'd grown up there.

Dad was a man of faith and devotion. His tall, tan presence—usually with a smile—brought a lot of trust. His brown eyes were anything but dull as they often twinkled while telling a story.

His congregation was about 300 people strong and the largest in our rural area. The church building sat prominently on top of a small hill. Behind it was a picturesque cemetery dotted with headstones large and small, modest and ornate.

When I was a child, my father would take me on walks through the cemetery, stopping at various headstones, telling stories about the deceased. Some good and some...not so much.

He seemed to know everyone in our community, dead or alive, and they all respected him.

My mother was...well...different. He loved her, I loved her, but...I don't know. Her ivory complexion, green eyes, and red hair presented an appropriate pastor's wife, but I always felt a distance there, as if she was going through the motions. Not connecting with me or anybody. She just never seemed...authentic. Based on her interactions with other people, I was the only one who felt that way.

Dad built the tree house for me when I was seven. He poured his heart and soul into every nail of my little fort. I suspect he wanted to do something special for his only child. A place away from the loving eyes of his parents. And I cherished it.

The most special part of it for me was the stained-glass window, fashioned together from bits and pieces of the remnants of the one at the church. Several years ago, a tornado had torn through the community and damaged the church building, but some of the stained glass had survived.

I really liked how it faced west and shined warm rays of colorful light throughout the tree house as the sun began to set. There's a purple glass cross kind of jigsaw-puzzled into the middle, surrounded by more colorful glass pieces. Under it, my father built a wooden shelf holding a candle and an old leather-bound Bible. On the inside cover, he inscribed: *God bless this little tree house.*

At dinner, Dad would sit at the head of the table, blessing our meal, then sharing stories about his day. They were always inspiring and told in a positive tone—even the bad ones. To me, he was an unbreakable, broad-shouldered man.

My mother would sit and listen, smiling, asking questions. But to me, it seemed...for lack of a better word...fake. I hated to think or feel such things about my own mother, but there was a phoniness there that, for some reason, my father didn't see. Or maybe he ignored it.

After dinner, I was overflowing with curiosity.

I crossed the road and snuck through the darkening woods, down to Mr. Wendorf's house.

Did Jimmie really shoot Mr. Wendorf? What if he did? What should I do?

It was time to find out.

Wendorf lived alone without any family that I could recall.

There were signs posted all around his property.

NO TRESPASSING – KEEP OUT.

I vividly remember a couple years back, being younger and more foolish. Jimmie and I would sneak through the woods onto his property. We'd then crawl on our bellies into his garden to take a cantaloupe. Then we would rush back into the dark woods, and when we were sure we were clear, we would go back into the tree house to eat it.

One night, Jimmie was leading the way, crawling up to the edge of the garden before stopping.

He whispered back to me: "The lights and TV are on in the living room."

What we didn't know, but soon found out, was that Mr. Wendorf had camouflaged himself, lying still and flat along the ground, hidden under the vines of the cantaloupe planted along the edge of the garden.

As we began to crawl forward, side-by-side, something grabbed Jimmie's leg.

"Let go of my leg," Jimmie whispered at me.

I whispered back, "I'm not touching your leg."

Then something firmly grabbed my ankle.

My heart jumped into my throat as I lay frozen.

Then the hand let go, and Mr. Wendorf sprung up holding a sawed-off shotgun, pumping it into action. He screamed: "Get off my property, you little bastards!"

Both Jimmie and I scrambled to our feet, screaming at the top of our lungs, running, stumbling over rocks and fallen branches back into the dark woods.

We not only heard the shotgun go off, but when I looked back to see if he was chasing us, I saw the blaze of sparks blasting out its muzzle as he fired a warning shot up into the sky.

"Oh my God!" I screamed.

"Run!" Jimmie screamed even louder. "RUN!"

Once back up into the tree house, we both swore we would never step foot back on his property again. I never had. And I thought Jimmie wouldn't either.

But I guess he did.

Now, I'd broken my own promise and cautiously approached Mr. Wendorf's house.

The lights were on in the living room, and I could hear the TV chattering.

Getting down onto my hands and knees, I slowly crawled around the back of the house.

I saw his pickup truck was still parked in the same spot.

I lifted my head up to look through the living room window. Surprisingly, it was open, and I could hear the talking on the TV very clearly.

Peeking into the living room, I could see Mr. Wendorf laying back in his recliner with his bare feet hanging just over the end. He had a blanket over him.

His mouth was open. His bald head seemed to shine slightly. Just above his right ear, I saw a nasty-looking reddish-brown crust that had oozed out and down the side of his head.

Was that a...bullet hole? It was gross.

I saw his right arm hanging over the side of the recliner, and on the floor was a pistol.

I stared, taking it in. It looked like he'd decided to shoot himself.

A shiver flooded over me as goose bumps popped up all over my skin.

Jimmie was right...he was dead.

The next morning, the bus rolled by Mr. Wendorf's house.

Nothing was different.

Only I knew it wasn't.

Mr. Wendorf was dead in his recliner with the TV on.

Jimmie claimed he'd shot him in his head.

The bus stopped, but Jimmie didn't get on.

CHAPTER 2

After school, I went up into the tree house.

That Mr. Wendorf hadn't been found was probably not surprising. Nobody in the area would probably care if he was dead.

But I cared.

I might not care as much if he had passed away in his sleep, but being shot in the head and having my friend claim to be involved in it?

I sat and pondered. Part of me wanted to call the police and leave an anonymous tip. Part of me wanted to tell my father. And part of me wished I didn't know it happened at all.

But I did.

I needed to talk with Jimmie and tell him I saw Mr. Wendorf dead in his recliner. I also needed to ask him why he wasn't at school today.

Then I heard my mother's voice, snapping me out of my thoughts. *"It's time for dinner."*

The relationship I had with my parents was...okay. I was much closer with my dad, but he spent so much time ministering to the congregation of the church that it was a treat when he was actually home. He obviously cared about me, often taking walks with me during his limited free time, asking me questions about my day, school, friends, etc.

Sometimes I'd help him at the church, setting up for events or cleaning out a room. But even that was limited. Still, I felt his love, and his awkward attempts to show it made me feel good.

My mother...she was much more distant. I don't know why. She would do what I guess you could call the typical motherly things—cooking meals, doing laundry, putting a bandage on my scraped knee...but it...how do I put this? There wasn't a feeling of love attached to it. She just did it. I got a better feeling from Emma, the housekeeper at the Kraus farm. Not that she did stuff any better or different, but she had a warmth.

My mother didn't have that. She never asked how I was doing, what was going on. Even when I was sick, she didn't do much. She'd bring me water or cough syrup with only the advice that I'd "get over it."

It wasn't a bad relationship. There just wasn't much of one at all.

Lying in bed, *What to do?* still going through my head, I tried to focus on Jimmie. I hadn't hung out with Jimmie or at his house much while growing up. We were more neighbors than friends, until last year when he saw the tree house. He'd asked if he could check it out and pretty much hung out with me nearly every day since. He even went in the tree house alone when I was working at the Kraus farm.

I'd never even met Jimmie's parents. I only remembered seeing his dad from a distance while he had the hood up, working on his semi-truck. Being a long-distant truck driver, he was away most all the time, and when he was home and not working on his truck, Jimmy said he was mostly napping.

Jimmie's mother, on the other hand, frequented the local taverns, enjoyed smoking her cigarettes, listening to country music, and drinking beer out of a brown bottle.

I tossed and turned, unable to sleep, all these odd thoughts running through my head.

At 3:14 am, somebody started beating on our front door.

I rushed out of bed to the door, and my dad was already there.

Mr. Kraus stood on the porch in panic. He's technically an old man—I didn't know if he's older than Mr. Wendorf, but his weathered complexion, bushy eyebrows, white wispy hair, usually under a well-worn baseball cap, put him, I would guess, in his seventies.

"Sam, help," he said, out of breath. "The Wendorf house...it has gone up...in a blaze of fire. I called...9-1-1."

Dad and I got on our shoes and jumped into my father's car, racing down the road.

The lights of the emergency vehicles were blinking and spinning, illuminating the entire area. The only thing brighter was the wall of flames engulfing the old house. They were higher than the nearby treetops. Even from where we stood on the road, the heat was unbearable, and we had to keep stepping back further and further.

One of the policemen noticed us and trotted over.

"Oh, hello, Pastor Douglas. Do you live nearby?"

"Just down the road."

"Do you know whose home this is?"

"Mr. Wendorf. I'm sorry, I don't know his full name."

"Benjamin," Mr. Kraus said. "Ben."

The policeman made a note. "Did he live alone, or could there be other people here?"

"No, he lives here alone," Mr. Kraus said.

The crackling blaze was too intense for the firemen to enter the house, but they aimed their hoses as best they could to not only knock down the flames but to spray down the surrounding area, keeping the flying embers from lighting fire to the trees.

The house creaked and groaned loudly as it began to crumble down upon itself.

"Do you see Mr. Wendorf here?" the young policeman asked.

My father and Mr. Kraus looked around, then shook their heads. There were only us, the firefighters, and the police. I pretended to look around as well, but I knew the truth. I knew where Mr. Wendorf was.

Looking around was when I noticed Jimmie standing at the edge of the woods. The light from the fire had illuminated him. No one noticed but me.

Then he vanished.

The firemen did their best, and it took them a little over an hour before they had nothing left but a smoldering heap of ashes contained within a stony foundation.

Hours later, heading out the door to catch the school bus, I noticed Jimmie's bicycle was leaning up against the tree beneath the tree house.

I climbed up to see Jimmie looking like he'd just woken up after spending the night there. "Hey. You okay?"

He nodded, rubbing his eyes.

"Did you burn down Wendorf's house?"

He shook his head. "No," Jimmie said firmly.

"I saw you in the woods."

He didn't say anything for a minute. Then: "I know you don't believe me, but I didn't start the fire."

I took a deep breath. "I snuck down to Wendorf's house and saw him dead in his recliner."

Jimmie tilted his head and stared back me. "I told you."

"You said you killed him. But the gun was by his right arm, and there was a bullet wound on the right side of his head."

Jimmy nodded. "I snuck in. You know, to look around. He was sleeping in his chair, and I saw the pistol on the end table next to him. That's when he suddenly woke up."

"Then what happened?"

"He grabbed the gun and put the barrel to his head. I jumped forward to knock it away, and that's when the gun went off. His hand fell away, and I was left holding the gun."

"Why were you in his house in the first place?"

He paused. "I was hungry; sometimes getting two servings at school isn't enough. That's when I saw him, then the gun. But that's when he woke up and literally scared the shit out me! Everything happened so fast... it was all just a blur. Then I grabbed his keys, ran out of the door, and took off in his pickup truck for a while before returning it."

"Why would he wake up and then shoot himself in the head? Why did you nail that bullet casing into the tree?" I asked, pointing at the bark. "It's not making sense."

Jimmie shook his head. "I'm here because I trust you. You did sneak down to Mr. Wendorf's house to see for yourself. You saw the gun; you saw him dead. You know, I'm telling the truth...right?"

"Okay then. Why weren't you at school today?"

"My mother took me to the DMV to take my road test. She said it was the only day she could take me," Jimmie said.

"Did you pass?"

After deciding to hide Jimmie's bike in the woods and skip school for the day, we needed more time to think this all through.

Mom and Dad had gone to visit someone in the hospital, so I went into the house to grab some leftovers for Jimmie.

He scarfed it all down—the pot roast, potatoes, carrots, and home-made bread my mother had made.

"Why did you come here and not go back home?"

13

"My mother didn't come home last night," he said, sort of muffled by a large bite of bread. "The electricity was shut off again, and I hate staying alone."

"Does that happen often?"

"More than I would like to say."

He turned and looked away, probably out of both guilt and embarrassment. Then he suddenly broke into tears and couldn't stop.

I didn't know what to say or do, so I did nothing.

He curled into the corner and cried himself to sleep.

I went back into the house and grabbed a blanket and pillow.

He was out like a light.

I sat against the wall of the tree house. I still had a lot of questions. I felt he hadn't told me everything, and I needed to know. At least his story explained why Mr. Wendorf's pickup truck wasn't parked where it usually was parked.

I considered Jimmie's not-so-normal life. It didn't excuse him from claiming he'd murdered Wendorf in cold blood.

So, I sat wondering: *Did he really kill Mr. Wendorf?*

Jimmie slept most of the day.

I heard a car pull into driveway, park, open, and shut its door.

I peeked through a crack between the boards to see who it was. It was my mother. She went into the house.

I woke Jimmie up just before the time the bus would normally be dropping us off. We both snuck down, darting off into the woods.

Jimmie jumped onto his bike and peddled off, while I circled around and waited for the bus to go by before starting to walk up the gravel driveway.

Mother was inside, busy making dinner.

As I came in, she never looked up from what she was stirring.

"Dinner will be ready soon."

"Okay."

I went to my bedroom, sitting on the edge of the bed for a couple minutes before going back outside, up into the tree house.

I sat and thought some more, my imagination trying to fill in the gaps of Jimmie's story. *"It's time for dinner."*

At school the next morning, I saw Jimmie coming down the hall. I waved at him, and I accidentally brushed against a girl passing by. She stumbled a little, and the next thing I knew, the guy she was walking with grabbed me by the throat and pushed me against the lockers.

It was Robert Schultz, the guy who had tried to beat up Jimmie the other day.

He suddenly recognized me, let go of me, and pointed at my face.

"Don't do that again," he said, walking away.

When I looked around, Jimmie was gone.

Just before the bus dropped me off, I stared out the window at the charred rubble that was once Mr. Wendorf's house.

Weirdly, his pickup truck now stood out parked in the same spot Jimmie had left it. Untouched by the flames.

After dinner, I went outside and saw Jimmie's bicycle lying on the ground under the tree house. I went up.

The candlelight was flickering off Jimmie's face.

"I'm sorry for not stepping in to help you at school," he said. "But he bullies me around all the time...steals my lunch money to buy his cigarettes."

15

"He steals your lunch money?"

"Not just me, but...yeah. He seems to get off on it."

"So why do you let him?"

"I don't let him, but I don't want to get punched the face again."

"Why weren't you on the bus this morning or after school?"

"I over-slept and missed the bus."

"But I saw you at school."

"I rode my bike."

I paused, thinking. "But that's nine miles each way. You know, a lot of what you say just doesn't make any sense."

"I know you're still wondering if I burnt down Wendorf's house, but... Dustin, it wasn't me. I didn't do it...I swear!"

Then he hurried past me, down the tree, then pedaled off into the woods.

I just sat there in the candlelight, not sure what to think.

CHAPTER 3

S aturday morning, I followed the smell of breakfast. My mother was flipping homemade pancakes and poking at the bacon. Dad sat at the head of the table sipping on his coffee, the newspaper propped open in front of him.

"Good morning," he said. "School should be out soon, eh?"

I took my seat. "Only a couple days left before summer break."

"What are you going to do?"

I shrugged. "Mr. Kraus will still need me."

"I heard the feed store is hiring."

I wrinkled my nose. "I don't know."

"They pay well. And you could work both." He folded the paper, showing me the headline.

BODY FOUND IN ASHES OF RICHMOND HOUSE FIRE. He laid the paper on the table and began to read.

"After a full investigation of the scene just outside the city limits of Richmond, the body of Benjamin Wendorf was discovered in the rubble. However, it has been determined by the Walworth County Coroner and Fire Chief Jeremy Brodsky that the cause of death of Mr. Wendorf was by a self-inflicted gunshot wound to the head. Chief Brodsky also said the fire was caused by an electrical short, possibly from the TV. The fire erupted twelve-to-twenty-four hours after Mr. Wendorf's death. In addition, the

Walworth County Coroner stated there has been no immediate family that has stepped forward at this time to claim the victim's remains."

Dad scratched his head. "I wonder how we can find any members of his family."

I was going to say, *Maybe someone will try to call him,* when I realized his phone would have burned up in the fire. But that gave me an idea.

"Maybe the phone company can have any calls he gets transferred to the police department."

Dad's eyes lit up. "Or here. I was thinking that if no one claims his body, I will."

"Why?"

"He'll need a proper funeral."

"Oh...yeah. Was he married?"

"No idea. If he was, she either left or passed on before we got here."

For the first time, Mother spoke up. "I never saw anyone go near that place except the mail man, and he stayed on the road."

My dad and I looked at each other, thinking the same thing.

"Maybe Sam delivered mail with a return address that might stand out," Dad said.

"He is a big snoop," I said.

Dad looked down his nose at me. "Just say he's curious, Dustin."

"Breakfast is ready!" Mother said, placing a plate in front of Dad and me.

"I'll also ask Mr. Kraus and Mr. Thomas if they might know someone," Dad said before bowing his head.

I thanked her as she sat down with her plate, and Dad said grace over the food.

With only few days of school left, I climbed up into my tree house thinking about working at the Kraus farm over the summer and dreaming about what type of vehicle I could buy with my savings. Dad said he would match me dollar for dollar to buy a used car or pickup.

But that was my dilemma—car or pickup?

Then I heard a muffled giggle, like that of a child, and splashing coming from outside.

That was odd. Dad had left. I thought Mom had left too.

I crawled across the floor and peeked through the boards.

I was surprised that, from my vantage point, I could see my mother moving around in the water of our above-ground pool.

Nearby in the water was a man. A man who was not my father.

Later that day, after Sam the postman didn't recall a single piece of mail with a return address that looked like it could be from family, my dad's "investigation" lead him to discover Mr. Wendorf had a stepsister. The police had already forwarded any calls to Mr. Wendorf's phone to their desk, but they said no one had called. No one cared.

A couple days later, seven people sat in the wooden pews of the church—Mr. and Mrs. Kraus, their housekeeper Emma, Mr. Thomas, a girl about my age, and me. The seventh person—who I was a bit surprised to see—was Jimmie.

Another surprise was someone I didn't see, my mother. Although I guess that's really not a surprise. If she didn't know the deceased, she didn't show up.

My father read scriptures and lamented the sad passing of a lonely old man, who Jimmie claimed was involved in his death. He didn't say that part about Jimmie, but I thought it.

The urn filled with Mr. Wendorf's remains sat atop a marble pillar like some kind of trophy. I wore my black suit and slacks—Dad had said I didn't need to wear a tie. I was relieved since I always forgot how to tie it. Everyone else wore black, except Jimmie, who had on a green T-shirt and denim shorts.

I heard a shuffling sound behind me and turned my head slightly to take a look. Only checking peripherally, all I knew was it was a lady.

I tried but couldn't shake the vision of Mr. Wendorf lying dead, body burning up in his recliner. What was now going through Jimmie's mind while he sat at the man's funeral? A man he had witnessed commit suicide.

But that brought the other question I've already myself asked a hundred times: *Why did Jimmie claim to kill him?*

When my father finished, he asked if anyone would like to say anything. Mr. Thomas stood up and shared a few kind words about being childhood friends. Then, he sat back down.

After a brief moment, my father closed the Bible and nodded. Mr. and Mrs. Kraus, Emma, Mr. Thomas, the girl, and the lady sitting behind me stood and began filing out.

I turned and asked Jimmie if he knew who the girl and older woman were.

"I never seen the old lady," Jimmie said, "but the girl is Abby. She lives down the road, at the Meyer Estate."

Abby looked rather—how should I put this? Farm girl-plain. Long dark brown hair wore in a bun, brown eyes, wearing what looked like a homemade dress. Not unattractive, but not exceptional.

"How come I haven't seen her at school?"

He shrugged. "I only seen her maybe two or three times and talked with her only once while I rode my bike down by the river. She was walking with another girl, and they asked if I knew which one of the trails would take them into Richmond."

The talk at school was buzzing about summer break.

I was still debating...car or pickup? A car is more comfortable, but you can get more stuff done with a pickup. A car is more attractive, and I bet the girls would prefer it. Not that they're lining up to hang out with me. But as a junior...with a driver's license...

Yeah, still probably not.

Again, I didn't see Jimmie on the bus, but I did see him at lunch in the cafeteria, heading back for seconds.

The last day of school while passing by the former Wendorf residence, I noticed...the pickup was gone. Where did it go? Since Wendorf didn't seem to have family, who took it?

When the bus came up to Jimmie's house, there was no Jimmie, so it kept going. When it pulled into the school parking lot, it was hard to miss all the local police and county sheriff's vehicles parked everywhere.

We stood up to get off the bus, but the door didn't open until a police detective showed up. He got on the bus, stood at the front, looking somber, eyes scanning everyone.

"I'm Detective Osborne, and we're going to need you all to go directly to the gymnasium. One of your fellow students has been killed, and we'll need to talk to each of you. If you wish, you can call your parents..."

It didn't take long for word to make it around. Before we even entered the gym, we'd heard Robert Schultz had been shot and killed.

That was the guy who had bullied Jimmie. Who'd grabbed me in the hallway.

The crime scene behind the school by the baseball practice field was cordoned off with yellow crime scene tape. It wasn't until after lunch that it was my turn to be interviewed.

"Dustin Douglas?" a sheriff deputy asked me as I sat down. "And how old are you?"

"Fifteen. I'll be sixteen in a couple days."

"Did you know Robert Schultz?"

I had to decide what to tell him. I did know him. I'd had a couple of run-ins with him. What would the police think of that?

"Yeah, he was a bully," I said, deciding honesty was the best policy.

"A couple of your classmates said he pushed you into a locker the other day. What was that about?"

"I accidentally bumped into his girlfriend, and he got mad."

"Anything come of it?"

I shook my head. "No. Like I said, he was a bully."

The deputy stared at me for a few seconds, as if judging whether I was telling the truth.

"And do you know Jimmie Becker?"

"Yeah, he's a friend of mine."

"Did Robert ever bully Jimmie?"

"Yeah, Jimmie said he'd take his lunch money. Stupid stuff like that."

"How about a boy named Rusty Appleby?"

"I've seen him around but don't really know him."

"I am told Jimmie Becker is not at the school right now."

I didn't know how to react to that, so I just said: "Oh, really?"

"Neither is Rusty."

I shook my head.

"We were told that, apparently, Robert caught Rusty talking with his girlfriend Connie by the baseball practice field. Robert confronted Rusty and become agitated, and a fight broke out. Jimmie jumped in to help." He paused, watching me.

"And now, both Rusty and Jimmie are gone."

While riding home on the bus, I couldn't stop wondering what had happened to Mr. Wendorf's pickup truck. And did Jimmie have anything to do with it?

After getting off the bus, I put my stuff in my room and then rode my bike over to Jimmie's house. No one was home. The place appeared abandoned.

Weird. Where did they go? And when?

I noticed a pile of old furniture and trash tossed by the road's edge... and an orange and black FOR RENT sign posted in the front yard.

I hopped off my bike to peek into the windows. My impression was correct—the house was empty.

Jimmie and his mom and dad were really gone!

I went back home and climbed up into the tree house.

"It's time for dinner."

My father talked about the shooting at the school.

"I was interviewed," I said, "but really don't know anything other than what I heard about Robert getting into a fight with Rusty. And Jimmie jumped in to break it up. That's what the policeman said."

"I heard a janitor found Robert's body," Dad said. "Shot to death."

I nodded. "That's what I heard too."

"When was the last time you saw Jimmie?"

"Yesterday, at lunch." I frowned. "I rode my bike down to his house today, and it was empty. There's a 'For Rent' sign and trash piled high in the front yard by the road."

"I thought that might happen. The Beckers were renting that place, and the owner told me just the other day he was going to have them evicted at the end of the school year."

"Why?" I asked.

"He said they were four months behind in rent."

Then Dad went back to talking about Robert Schultz and why anyone would want to shoot an innocent kid like that.

He's not so innocent, I thought. But I kept that to myself for now.

After dinner, I returned to the tree house, drifting off, thinking *Where did Jimmie go?* The colorful evening light reflected through the stained-glass window.

The next morning, my first day of summer break, I reached over to turn off the buzzing alarm. 6:00 am. I'd promised Mr. Kraus to help bale hay at 7:00.

After a day in the hot humid June sun, I was exhausted. All I wanted to do was go home, take a shower, eat, and go to bed. So, I took short cut through the woods.

As I approached the backyard, I noticed a flickering light coming through the stained-glass window in the tree house.

I leaned my bike up against the base and climbed up its side.

I was surprised not to find Jimmie but instead the girl I had seen at Mr. Wendorf's funeral—Abby. She was sitting in the candlelight, hands over her face, crying.

"Are you okay?"

She didn't look up at me. "No!"

I paused, feeling awkward. I didn't know what to say or do.

She wiped at her face and looked at me.

"Your mother is about to do something terrible to your father and me."

I blinked several times.

My mother?

"What? What will she do?"

Abby sighed heavily and sniffed.

"I accidentally caught her this morning...down in the basement at the Meyer Estate. She was...she was smacking around one of the girls."

She paused to gauge my reaction.

I didn't react. I didn't know how to react.

"This wasn't the first time I saw something like that. I've seen her hitting and beating on the girls for no reason. One time, she was teaching me how to make homemade bread, and...well, from out of nowhere, she just yanked on my hair...she pulled hard. And then she backhanded me for not following her instructions...but I did! I did exactly what she said.

I pushed her away and asked her to please stop hurting me. But I could tell she was angry."

Her hand wiped her nose.

"So, after seeing how horrible she treated that girl today, I felt I had to tell somebody...so I went to the church, but your father wasn't there. When I came out of the church..." She shook her head as if to clear her head.

"When I came out of the church, your mother was waiting for me. There was...fire in her eyes. She came at me, grabbed me by my hair, and jerked me around to the side of the church. She said, 'What did you see? Did you tell anyone?'"

I had never seen my mother act that way...and yet, oddly, it didn't surprise me. "I told her I didn't know what she was talking about," Abby said. "That's when she slapped my face and called me a no-good little bitch. She said bad things would happen to me and to your father if he finds out."

She paused, as if to see whose side I was going to take.

But a familiar voice from below:

"It's time for dinner."

Abby froze, her eyes wide as if she'd heard the voice of evil. Then Abby reached into a pocket and pulled something out. "Jimmie asked me to give you this."

She handed me a folded-up piece of paper. Without saying another word, she hurried to the opening in the floor and disappeared, probably running off into the woods.

I stared at the opening in the floor, and that's when I noticed a hammer lying next to it. I saw another bullet casing had been pounded into the bark...next to the other one Jimmie had nailed into the tree.

I stuffed the note in my pocket and headed down.

CHAPTER 4

I unfolded the piece of paper Abby had given to me. It appeared to be some kind of map with no words…just dotted lines and three X's that seemed to begin at the tree house that led out into the woods. I'd have to wait until morning to follow it.

At dinner, I considered what Abby had told me while watching my mother. She acted perfectly normal. For her.

Mother had been a volunteer at the Meyer Estate since it opened fifteen years before. I was just a baby at the time.

I decided to say something, to ask questions. Maybe it would make my mother have second thoughts.

"You know the girl at the funeral?" I asked, looking at my dad. "Who was she?"

"Abby Meyer is her name. After, Mr. Thomas explained Mr. Wendorf's involvement, she asked if he would take her to Mr. Wendorf's funeral so she could pay her respects and show her gratitude. Mr. Wendorf was the one who anonymously donated a large sum of money in an effort to help take care of baby Abby and the property at the time until the Meyer Estate Foundation was established. She was involved in a horrific accident where her mother, father and three of her sisters were tragically killed when they were hit in their car by a train after a railroad crossing malfunctioned. Abby was the sole survivor and was three months old at the time. In an effort to care for the orphaned child, I got the community together to help provide care, food, and money shortly before a foundation was launched.

"Abby's father, Mr. Meyer was an inventor who developed a new lightweight material stronger than Kevlar. He sold the technology to the US military, and his estate had an estimate net worth of $4.5 million. Plus, attorneys were successful in settling out of court with the railroad company for $15 million on behalf of the orphaned baby Abby.

"The lawyers then drafted formal papers for the Meyer Foundation and placed the twenty-acre property under the protection of the Meyer Historical Society, a non-profit created to supervise and budget the maintenance to the property and to provide care and guardianship for the surviving child.

"The board members also set up and opened the estate to take in other orphaned girls within the area and to help selected females to get rehabilitated from the nearby female prison Sugar Creek Correctional Facility. Last I heard, there were...?"

He stopped and looked at Mother.

"How many girls are living there?"

"Seven," she said.

Dad nodded. "They're assigned household duties and attend classes designed to advance their education, prepping them for the day they leave. The Meyer Foundation gives each 'graduating' girl a scholarship to the University of Wisconsin. Does that help?"

"Yeah, thanks. I just wondered why I'd never seen her before."

"The girls who live at the Meyer Estate mainly stay on the property." Continuing, Dustin's dad asked, "Well, I have a question for you. Why do you think Jimmie would be eluding the police?"

"You mean for killing Robert?"

Dad looked at me curiously. "I don't think you heard. The news said Rusty Appleby was found dead from an apparent suicide."

My stomach seemed to roll over. "Oh no."

"Apparently, he left a handwritten letter stating he did not kill Robert Schulz but knew who did."

"Oh my gosh. Did it say who?"

"No, that's the problem. And Jimmie Becker has gone missing, so now the police have placed an 'all points bulletin' out for him."

I sat quietly thinking for a moment. "It's hard to say if Jimmie was capable of doing something like that."

The next morning, I was coming downstairs for breakfast when someone knocked on the door.

I stopped and peeked through the blinds.

Two men in suit and ties were standing there.

I opened the door but didn't say anything.

"Is Pastor Douglas here?"

Before I had a chance to speak, my father walked up behind me. "Yes, I'm Pastor Douglas. How can I help you?"

"Mr. Douglas, we have a warrant for your arrest in the death of Abby Meyer." Me and my father said at the same time: *"What?"*

"Can you step out onto the porch please? Do you have any weapons on you?"

The rest was like a weird TV dream. There was the whole "You have the right to remain silent" thing as handcuffs were placed my father's wrists.

"But there must be a horrible mistake," Dad said.

Then they turned, walked my father out, and stuffed him into the back of a sedan.

I stood in shock, just watching.

Behind me, I heard Mother say: "Your father is in really big trouble." Her tone was flat, impassive.

I turned to look at her, and she just looked...blank. No emotion. No surprise. No anger.

Just...nothing.

Then she turned and walked into the kitchen.

I went up to the tree house, trying to figure out what to do.

Abby was dead?

Rusty was dead.

Robert was dead.

Mr. Wendorf was dead.

Jimmie was missing.

Dad had been arrested.

Who could I turn to?

I heard a car door slam shut and its engine turn on.

I peeked through the boards to see my mother sitting behind the wheel of the car. She backed out of the driveway and sped off down the road.

Think, Dustin. Think.

Nothing at first...then...

First, I go to the Kraus farm and explain I need to take the day off to help my father with something that has unexpectedly come up.

Second, I need to figure out Jimmie's map.

And third, find out what happened to Abby...and why they think my father had anything to do with it.

Mr. Kraus said I could take the day off and then asked if everything was all right.

Instead of answering, I thanked him and said I had to go.

Back at the tree house, I pulled out the map. I thought I'd take a chance and head off into the woods toward the first of the three X's.

It took longer than I thought, winding through the woods close to the riverbank and then to a mature oak tree on a hill overlooking the water.

I stood there looking around and noticed a stone that was just sitting in the middle of a small pile of dirt. It looked like it had been placed there.

I knelt down and began sweeping away the dirt, digging down. I soon felt something round and smooth. It was the top of a jar.

I pulled it out and saw there was something inside. I unscrewed the lid and removed a lot of bills—$20, $50, and $100—tightly rolled up.

I felt in the dirt again and found another, then another—three glass mason jars in total.

No note or anything. Just money.

I looked around to make sure no one else was there and put the jars back into the ground and covered them up, replacing the stone as a marker.

Now I was really curious about the second X.

It was a little bit more difficult to locate, but under another mature oak tree about fifty yards away, I noticed another stone. Sure enough, there were five more jars, along with a plastic container the size of a rectangle cake pan.

After digging them out, I again found all the jars stuffed full of money. The plastic container was full to the brim with gold and silver coins. It was heavy, so I left it in place.

I replaced the lid and re-laid the jars back into the dirt. I covered them up again.

The third X led me to the far back corner of Mr. Wendorf's property.

Under the oak tree was an old rusted greenish-blue farm tractor next to a four-row plow overgrown with rust, weeds, and vines.

I looked around for another stone or mound of dirt when I heard car doors shut off in the distance.

I hurried behind the tree and hid, hearing muddled talk getting closer.

I was hiding about forty yards from where Mr. Wendorf's house used to be and peeking around the tree trunk when I saw three men and a woman. They were carrying black duffel bags. One of them had a camera, and the woman carried a clipboard. It looked like they were all dressed in navy-blue police clothing. Something official.

I heard them talking about a crime scene—two fishermen had discovered something just over the hill by the bank of the river. They then walked off over a hill and out of sight.

I reopened the map to confirm I was in the correct spot. Then I noticed a flat rock by the base of the tree, not far from my feet. I reached down to move the stone, and under it was a plastic baggie. Inside appeared to be a note.

CHAPTER 5

My hand shook slightly as I reached inside the plastic baggie. I slid out the folded piece of paper, and I quickly saw it was a part note, part map.

> *Dustin*
>
> *Darkened by confusion, it's time for me to discover the truth.*
>
> *Jimmie*

The little map had a set of dots ending with a single X.

No time like now, I thought.

The dots looked like they were right in Mr. Wendorf's garden and led me toward a pile of old boards stacked alongside a free-standing but dilapidated tool shed. As I reached the tiny building, I saw something out of the corner of my eye—a white van pulling into the driveway behind the other two vehicles already there.

I quickly slid around the corner of the shed to hide.

I peeked to see two men dressed in black get out and open the rear doors of the van, then slide out a gurney. They rolled it off in the direction to where the earlier investigators had gone down by the river.

Once they were out of sight, I continued, going inside the tool shed. It was dark and musty, but I spotted the corner of a wooden door, like a trap door, lying flat on the ground. I lifted what turned out to be a hinged wooden storm door surrounded by a concrete frame. It creaked and squeaked as it opened, but I could just make out concrete stairs that lead down to another doorway. Was it a storm cellar?

Carefully stepping down the stairs in the dark, I managed to open the second door. Just inside, it felt clammy and smelled stale and even more musty. It took a while for my eyes to adjust, but the room seemed to be about 10 x 12, 8 foot in height. One wall was lined with sturdy wooden shelves nailed together using what looked like re-purposed boards.

On the shelves were nothing but jar after jar—stuffed full of money—from left to right, top to bottom, six jars deep.

Along another wall, the shelves were stacked with plastic containers like the one I had just discovered outside. There must have been hundreds. In the middle of the room, there was a small, old farmhouse-style dropleaf table with a single chair, all covered with dust. No one had been down here in a long time.

All of this must belong to Mr. Wendorf! It has to be his.

I heard the slamming of vehicle doors from above, followed by the sound of their engines starting up and the crunching of gravel under their tires as they slowly rolled away.

I hurried up the stairs and peeked out, seeing the three vehicles pulling out of Mr. Wendorf's driveway turn onto the road heading toward Richmond. I went back down, sitting on the bottom stair, trying to collect my scattered thoughts while studying the room filled with money.

How did Jimmie know about this?

That led me to wonder about Jimmie's disappearance—*Where did he go?*

I was overwhelmed and lost in this rapidly shifting world. People dying, disappearing, my mother accused of child abuse, and now my dad arrested for killing the girl who was abused.

After replacing the boards to the storm door, I headed back down to the river. It wasn't long before I found the yellow tape strung out between trees along with tiny orange flags sticking in the ground marking points of interest. A crime scene.

As I came closer to the taped-off area, I noticed in the dirt the outline of a human body, spray-painted white...and a dark patch of dirt in the middle.

Saturated with blood?

Suddenly, I felt light-headed and nauseous, everything catching up with me. I turned, vomited into a small grassy area, then began running as fast as possible through the woods, back up into the tree house.

I was haunted by the thought of someone's body lying dead down by the riverbank. I had walked right past that exact area earlier...and there wasn't anybody lying there. Unless I missed it. But how would I do that?

Maybe I was focusing so close on Jimmie's map, I didn't notice the body.

No! I would have noticed a body lying there!

How did a body get in that area?

And whose body could it have been?

I heard a vehicle pulling into the driveway, and I looked down through the boards.

A green pickup truck. Mr. Kraus. He parked, then got out and started walking up to our front door. He had on his usual bib overalls and slip-on round-toed leather work boots.

I hurried down, and as he was about to knock, I walked around the corner of the house.

"Oh, hi, Dustin. Is your father home?"

"No."

"Do you know where he is?"

I had to pause to consider what to say. How much should I tell him?

Mr. Kraus noticed my hesitation. "Do you know where your father is?"

I looked away. "Yes."

Mr. Kraus placed his hand on my shoulder. "What has happened?"

"Two men came this morning and said they are taking him to the county jail."

"Why?"

"They said...they said for the murder of...the murder of Abby Meyer."

Mr. Kraus frowned. "Do you know where your mother is?"

"No. She left right after they took him."

"Okay, I heard something about all that," Mr. Kraus said. "I am here to help you figure this out."

"My mother said...my father is in really big trouble. Why would she say that?"

Mr. Kraus didn't answer right away. I could tell he was thinking, trying to decide what to do. Then he nodded.

"Come on, let's go to town to find your father."

He led me down, and we hopped into the pickup truck.

I had the feeling Mr. Kraus knew more than he was letting on.

We walked into the lobby of the county jail, and Mr. Kraus asked the female officer sitting behind the desk if we could see Sam Douglas.

"I'm sorry, Mr. Douglas has been placed in isolation under direction of District Attorney Michael Corbett. You'll have to make arrangements through him in order to gain visitation."

We drove to Mr. Corbett's office, but it had a sign hanging in the window.

Closed – In Court.

"I don't think it's good for you to be alone right now," Mr. Kraus said as we drove back. "You can stay with us."

"I appreciate that, but I'd rather stay at home."

"Okay," he said as we pulled into the driveway. "If you change your mind, just come on over."

I thanked him again and got out.

He backed out, then drove away.

I walked up to the front door, but...I was puzzled...because the door was locked. It's never locked.

I walked over to where a spare key was hidden. But it wasn't there. I was locked out of my home.

I walked around to the back door by the kitchen. Locked. I tried some of the windows.

Locked.

I climbed up into the tree house and lit the candle to wait until my mother came home.

She didn't come home that day.

I lay awake a good part of the night, thinking about Jimmie and his not-so-normal life and the emptiness he must have felt sleeping alone in the tree house.

I thought of my mother hurting Abby.

I thought of my father being arrested for the murder of Abby

I thought of the weird treasure hunt with money here, there, and underground.

I eventually drifted off and woke up on the floor of the tree house.

I looked outside, but still no Mother.

I folded the blanket and placed it and the pillow back in the corner.

My stomach growled.

I considered what to do.

I jumped on my bike and pedaled off.

I stood looking down at the taped-off area by the riverbank. Could that really be the outline of Abby's body? A girl I only briefly knew. And now she's gone.

I saw a trout fisherman coming down the river in his waders, waving his fly rod back and forth. On one of his strokes, he noticed me. He waved and made his way over.

"Good morning."

"Good morning," I said.

"This must be the spot everyone is talking about."

"What are they saying?"

"A girl was badly beaten, raped, and left to die."

"Who said that? Did they say who did it?"

"I heard Pastor Douglas, from the Believers Fellowship Church."

That feeling of being overwhelmed came back, so I picked up my bike and pedaled off without saying another word.

I raced to the church, rushing up the front stairs before noticing it was locked up with a chain and a padlock hanging from the handles. Stapled to the door was a piece of paper.

This building has been ordered closed until further notice. -- Judge Philip Dru.

I stood at the top of the stairs and looked out. I saw a van with a TV station logo, antenna up. A cameraman was filming a professionally-dressed woman talking into a microphone.

A car drove by with a middle-aged man, and he shouted, *"Pastor Douglas is a murderer!"*

This was not a good place to be, I decided.

I hopped on my bike and pedaled as fast as I could back to the tree house.

I kept thinking, thinking, thinking.

My father would never kill anybody.

My mother...well, I didn't know what to think.

I reached over and grabbed the Bible off the wooden shelf.

I stared at my father's handwritten message:

Bless this little tree house.

Yes, I decided. The little tree house did feel like it had been blessed. I was beginning to realize the tree house was not only providing a source of refuge but also what I felt was valuable knowledge, strength, and guidance.

My stomach groaned with emptiness, so I decided to get some money out of one of jars buried under the oak tree, and then I pedaled into town to get something to eat.

My route took me past the Meyer Estate, and my curiosity overran my appetite. I stowed my bike off the road.

I began sneaking through the woods looking for any sign of anyone—particularly my mother. I noticed a sheriff's vehicle in the driveway by what looked like the guest house.

I crouched around the trees and behind bushes, working my way toward the back.

I had never been on the Meyer property, and I noticed not just the small guest house but a fairly large garden, a detached four-car garage, and the three-story main house. All the structures were made out of a brownish-red brick with white-trimmed windows and doors.

As I snuck closer to the guest house, I could hear a steady moaning sound coming through an open window. I slowly peeked up over the sill of the window.

There was a bed with a naked woman entangled with a man; he was the same man I had seen in our pool. The woman turned her head slightly, eyes closed...and that's when I saw it was my mother.

I quickly slid myself down, wanting to melt into the ground. The moaning increased, as did the sound of heavy breathing.

I couldn't...I couldn't...I just slowly made my way back toward my bike.

I can't say I knew much about sex, but the vision of my mother having it with a strange man was all too much. And I was afraid the moaning sound would haunt me for a very long time.

As I rode into town, my mind was stuck on repeat, playing the sight and sound of my naked mother over and over.

CHAPTER 6

At Mary Lou's Diner, I was starved. I ordered a soda, a BLT with fries. It didn't seem like enough, but it was a start.

The restaurant was small but clean, and the waitress was busy going from table to table. But I hardly noticed, buried in my troubles.

Thankfully, the waitress broke me from my deep, dark thoughts as she served my food. It wasn't long before it was all gone.

Looking around, I saw many of the other diners had their noses in the newspaper. I could overhear the two men talking behind me, discussing the brutal murder of a young girl down by the river. They both had their opinions, but they were both certain Pastor Douglas—my father—was the killer.

The waitress slipped the bill on the table and said, "Thanks, sweetie."

After leaving a tip, I grabbed my bill and headed to the checkout. There, I saw today's headline of *The Richmond Times.*

PASTOR DOUGLAS ARRESTED FOR MURDER

It featured a black-and-white photo of my father. They had managed to find a picture that made him look cold and guilty, gripping the sides of the lectern during a Sunday service.

I set down a quarter and picked up a copy.

I pedaled as fast as I could back to the tree house, but the next thing I knew, there was a county sheriff's vehicle crawling alongside of me, its lights whirling blue and red. The front passenger window was down as the officer motioned to me to pull over and stop.

I guided my bike off the edge of the road while the cruiser came to a stop behind me.

My heart was beating fast, not just from pedaling so hard.

The officer got out of his car and placed his hat on his head. I saw he was carrying a small black leather flip notepad.

As my heart slowed, my brain began to race, wondering why I had been stopped.

"What's your name?"

I opened my mouth to answer, but I saw Mr. Kraus's pickup pulling off the edge of the road behind him. The officer turned to watch the truck park.

Mr. Kraus got out, coming up to us.

"Good morning, Officer Mullin. How are you today?"

"Fine," Mullin said flatly.

Mr. Kraus turned to me. "I was on my way over to pick you up." Being a bit puzzled, I didn't say anything back.

"May I ask what's going on, Officer Mullin?" Mr. Kraus asked.

"This young man fits the description of a missing child recently posted."

"Well, I think you can see you have the wrong child. This is Dustin, and he's certainly not missing. I've known him for many years."

The officer nodded his head, closed his notepad, and slid it back in his front uniform shirt pocket. "Very well. You two have a good day." He headed back to his cruiser.

Mr. Kraus looked at me. "Come on. We have things to do." Then he walked over to my bike and placed it in the back of his truck.

I got in the passenger seat as Mr. Kraus got behind the wheel.

"Glad I came along. The way things have been going, he might have taken you in."

A few minutes later, he drove up his long driveway and parked by the side of his house. "I think it's best if you stay with us until everything gets worked out. I don't things are safe." He paused. "I don't know what's going on...but something isn't right."

He got out and lifted my bike out of the bed. I guided it over to lean against the railing of the porch, then we entered his house.

Just inside, Mrs. Kraus was scooting across the kitchen floor, hunched over her walker she needed to use because of her deformed left leg. Her face blossomed into a warm smile, and her eyes sparkled from behind her wire-rimmed glasses when she saw me. She always looked sickly but had an upbeat personality.

"I've brought Dustin to stay with us until things get settled," her husband said.

In her delicate voice, Mrs. Kraus said: "You are welcome to stay as long as needed and please feel free to come and go as you wish."

I recalled my father sharing the incident a few years back when Mrs. Kraus was stricken with pneumonia after suffering a major stroke. She was in grave danger. My father prayed over her and comforted Mr. Kraus at the hospital, and he returned for many days and nights until Mrs. Kraus was released. Mrs. Kraus swore it was one of God's miracles that spared her life.

But the problem with her leg came from a side-effect of drinking contaminated water while on a mission trip to a small village in Nicaragua and contracting polio when she was seventeen.

"Emma," Mrs. Kraus said, "can you show Dustin to his room?"

Emma was sitting at the kitchen table sewing a button on a shirt. She was in her late fifties with a slender build, big smile, and brown eyes that always seemed wise.

She set down the garment and smiled at me. "Certainly."

I knew Emma lived in a small but cozy rustic tin-roofed log cabin that was within walking distance of the Kraus's farmhouse.

After Emma showed me to the bedroom, she said, "There is some homemade chicken dumpling soup simmering on the stove if you're hungry."

Then she returned to the kitchen.

I wanted to read the newspaper, but first, I wanted to go back to my tree house. So, I slipped away from the Kraus property, hopped on my bike, and rode off through the woods.

I was still deeply confused since I couldn't make any sense of anything—while at the same time, everything seemed to be eroding from under me.

As I approached the backyard, I saw several people standing in the driveway and others going in and out of the house.

Then I saw the tree-cutters truck, and attached to it was a two-wheel wood-chipper parked just off the driveway. Men in hardhats and safely glasses stood around the base of the tree house, looking up, pointing, planning their strategy to bring down my beloved refuge.

"STOP! STOP!" I screamed as I ran toward them.

The men quickly turned as I raced to them on my bike.

I skidded to a halt in front of them. "What's...going...on?" I asked, out of breath.

One of the men looked me up and down. "We were hired to cut down and remove this tree and the tree house. Who are you?"

"Dustin," I said. "And that's my tree house."

"I'm sorry, but we have a work order here."

I felt a bit of panic as my mind raced, not knowing what to do.

"How much?" I blurted out.

"How much what?"

"How much would it cost to stop you?"

The man holding a clipboard looked down at it, then back up. "We were hired for $500."

The man handed the clipboard over to me.

Before I could read it, a neatly dressed man approached. "What's going on?"

The tree-cutter said, "This young man asked us to stop."

The man in the suit looked at me. "So, may I ask who you are?"

"Dustin Douglas."

He paused as that sunk in. "You're the son of Pastor Douglas?"

"Yes."

"I'm Al Bennett of Bennett's Realty." He stuck out his hand to shake.

Still confused, I shook it.

"I was hired to get this property and house prepped and ready for sale."

"For sale? Who hired you?"

"Mrs. Douglas. She said it was due to all the pending expenses of your father's legal trouble."

I was stunned. My mother now wanted to help Dad?

Mr. Bennett continued: "Your mother was very precise in her instructions before signing the seller's contract."

"How much?"

Mr. Bennett frowned. "How much what?"

"How much are you selling the house for?"

"Eighty-five thousand."

"Do you have any offers?"

"No, not yet. I'm in the process of listing it."

"Okay, well, I'll pay you $85,000, and I'll pay these guys $1,000 NOT to cut down my tree!"

Then I ripped up the work order and tossed the pieces onto the ground.

Mr. Bennett clenched his lips, quickly spun around, and stormed off into the house.

I looked at the foreman who had been hired to cut down the tree. "If you wait here, I'll be back in a few minutes with your money."

He smirked at me, then shrugged.

I raced back through the woods to the hidden glass jars buried under the oak tree by the river. I removed a jar and counted out $1,000, and then stuffed the money into my front pants pocket before riding back to my home.

Huffing and puffing, I handed him the cash. He counted it, then turned, and they began repacking their ropes, ladders, and chainsaws, putting them into their truck; then they drove off.

Mr. Bennett rushed up to me, looking pissed off. "I called your mother, and she said she will *NOT* accept your offer!"

I suddenly felt very hot with anger. I felt like kicking good ol' Al Bennett hard enough to give him something to be pissed about. But I didn't.

Without saying a word, I turned my bike around and sped off.

Mr. Kraus was hunched over working on his tractor as I approached. He looked back over his shoulder to see me rushing up to him.

"Mr. Kraus, they were going to cut down the tree and remove my tree house. My mother is putting our house up for sale. I can't have that happen. My mother can't do this! She can't have it cut down. I don't know what to do! Please, I need your help—*please, please, please!*"

He wiped his hands on an old towel.

"Okay, get in the truck; we'll find out what's going on."

We got in the truck, and as we rolled up in front of my house, there was a bright red-and-white FOR SALE sign stuck in the yard.

I jumped out of the truck and ran over to the sign, rocking it back and forth, yanking it up out of the ground. I tossed the sign into the back of Mr. Kraus's truck before getting back in the cab.

"Dustin," Mr. Kraus said. "We don't have enough money to pay for a down payment on your house."

"How much?" I asked.

"How much...of a down payment?"

"Yes."

"Five to twenty percent is normally required."

"Mr. Bennett said the selling price is $85,000. So, I'll need..."

"Between roughly $4,000 and $15,000," Mr. Kraus said.

"I have enough to give you that...in CASH!"

Mr. Kraus cocked his head. "I don't pay you enough for that," he said.

"I...I have the money," I said, not explaining.

He squinted at me, then gave an abrupt nod of his head. He opened the pickup door and slid out of the driver's seat. He walked up to the house and opened the front door.

Now it was unlocked!

He disappeared into the living room.

While he made his phone call, I got on my bike and sped off to the secret stash of cash.

CHAPTER 7

When I got back, my pockets full of cash, Mr. Kraus was still in the house but came out a minute later.

He reached into the bed of the truck to pull out the realty sign. He then re-stuck it into the grass of the front yard.

"I talked to him on the phone, and he's coming back," Mr. Kraus said. "Best to keep the sign in place for now, but I think we can make a deal."

He looked at me very seriously.

"Are you sure you can get the money?"

I nodded. "Yep." I stuck my hand in my right jeans pocket and pulled out a wad of cash.

He looked at it, then at me, and sighed.

"Okay. I don't know where you got this, and I'm not sure I should ask."

"It's fine," I said.

An hour later, I found myself kneeling inside the tree house, looking through the boards, watching as Mr. Bennett's vehicle pulled into the driveway.

Bennett got out and approached Mr. Kraus standing by his truck.

After a brief handshake, both men began walking around the property, occasionally stopping to discuss things before moving on. Sometimes, they went out of my view.

But I saw Mr. Kraus point to the tree house and then Mr. Bennett writing on his paperwork. They then went in the house, staying in there for what seemed like hours. It was probably only fifteen or twenty minutes until they came back outside.

Mr. Bennett laid down the papers on the hood of the truck, flipping through the paperwork while the men talked for several more minutes. It appeared Mr. Bennett needed to make a phone call, as he gestured toward the house, then disappeared inside while Mr. Kraus stood looking through the papers.

Mr. Bennett returned, and they talked a little more while flipping through the paperwork.

Then, I saw Mr. Kraus reach into his back pants pocket.

But, instead of pulling out the cash I gave him, he pulled out a checkbook. Then he signed the contract, filled out a check, and handed it over to Mr. Bennett.

Mr. Bennett handed Mr. Kraus his copy of the contract and pocketed the check. Then he went to the rear of his car, popped open the trunk, and pulled something out. He walked to the sign stuck in the grass and placed a magnetic "Pending Sale" sign on it. He shook Mr. Kraus's hand again, then drove away.

Mr. Kraus walked toward the base of the tree house, and I heard him climbing up the side.

His head stuck up through the hole. "It's been a long time since I've been up into a tree house. This is much nicer than I remember!"

He pulled himself up and sat against the wall, legs stretched out in front of him. "Your dad did a fine job building this."

"Why didn't you give Mr. Bennett the cash I gave you?"

He didn't answer, instead pulling the Bible off its shelf, opening it to the first page.

"Bless this little tree house," he read out loud.

He smiled, closing the Bible and replacing it onto its shelf.

"Is that the same glass from the window of the church? Damaged during the tornado?"

"Yeah."

"I remember your father worked endless hours to raise the money to help all the families in need. And to rebuild the church. But I recall it was a substantial donation given by Mr. Wendorf that really helped the community and to complete the church. Of course, Wendorf gave anonymously, but your dad figured it out."

Back at the Kraus's, in the guestroom, under the covers, I found myself lying still in the darkness, absorbing my new surroundings.

The house was quiet, and the cool night air flowed gently through the screen window. The mattress was cozy, and the sheets, blanket, and pillows had the fresh scent of being air-dried outdoors.

Even though I was exhausted, my mind was still active.

I kept thinking of when I'd peeked over the windowsill, seeing Mr. Wendorf stretched out, lying dead in his recliner with his bare feet hanging off the end, the bullet hole in his head oozing brownish dry blood, the TV still on, a pistol by his side.

Next, it was a flashback from months earlier. Me, frantic, running away through the dark woods, looking back to see the bright blast and hearing the bang of Mr. Wendorf's shotgun as he fired, warning me and Jimmie.

Then came the intense heat radiating as me and my dad—along with Mr. Kraus—witnessed Mr. Wendorf's house go up in a blaze of fire...with me knowing Wendorf was inside...dead...and observing Jimmie's silhouette sneaking off in the distance.

Jimmie said he'd shot Mr. Wendorf in the head...but did he? And where was he now? Mr. Kraus saying it was Mr. Wendorf who'd given a large sum of money anonymously to help aid the many families and to help my father to finish rebuilding the church. Why would Mr. Wendorf do this?

The end of the school year...and so much had happened. Three, four people dead. Wendorf, Robert, Rusty, Abby. Dad in jail. Abby crying in the tree house, handing me the map she said was from Jimmie. Mother... well...with some strange man. Also locking me out and putting our home up for sale.

But something told me many of these things had been unfolding for years.

I didn't even know what day of the week it was.

I suddenly felt hot and sticky, confused, with one image playing over and over in my head. It felt like my mind was being poisoned by evil.

Who was that naked man in bed with my mother? Holding onto her as she passionately moaned in rhythm?

Enough! Enough of this!

I stood, took off my pajamas, and quietly got dressed. I tip-toed over to raise the screen and slide myself out the window. Once outside, I grabbed my bike and pedaled off into the moonlit night.

I laid my bike on its side just in the woods, then scurried across the grass, up the boards, and into the tree house. I found the matches and lit the candle. I sat back, catching my breath, and noticed a folded piece of paper protruding just under the cover of the Bible.

I slid the piece of paper out and unfolded it. I found the most beautiful artistic cursive writing. Never had I seen such fantastic penmanship.

Dear God,

I never wanted to be the person You see now.

Please help me...I feel nothing...

Please forgive me and show me who I am...who I am supposed to be.

The candlelight was calming, and I felt safe, away from the outside world. Like every night, I said my nightly prayers.

But I found my words jumbled...and my thoughts unclear. I paused, trying to find what I wanted to say.

Then, without warning, something happened that I'd never experienced before...

I began to hear a voice.

It sounded similar to my father's, only deeper in tone.

I lifted my head, shocked, and my eyes sprang open to look around. I was alone. And the words I heard...were gone.

After a moment, I bowed my head again and closed my eyes. I found it difficult to re-focus.

Again, the mysterious voice took control and reshaped my prayer.

I don't remember the exact words, but the voice began describing the moral strength one must have to battle evil forces...and to help protect the vulnerable and the weak.

The prayer felt uplifting and insightful. Hopeful. Calm. Still, its message was dark and disturbing in its description of how blindly we all can fall prey to evil and its bloodthirsty lies.

Amen, the voice said.

And it was over.

I said, "Amen."

I reached over to lay out the blanket and pillow, then blew out the candle.

Finally, I was at peace.

I drifted off to sleep as the calmness and peace of the night enveloped the tree house.

I was awoken into the darkness by the sound of crunching gravel. A vehicle had entered the driveway.

I peeked and saw it pull in with its light off. The engine shut off, and two car doors softly closed. The voices were hard to make out. But as they drew closer, I could begin to hear their conversation.

I could see it was two male police officers dressed in their uniforms, each carrying a red plastic gas can with a yellow spout.

They stopped at the bottom short of the tree.

I felt my heart begin to pound faster in my chest.

I recognized one of the men. Officer Mullin. The one who had pulled me over while I was on my bike. The other man, a bit portly, I hadn't seen before.

"Do you really think he'll give me a promotion?" the portly officer asked Mullin. "You've been working for the department for three years now. He said he would promote you after this...right?"

"That's what he said. What's the big deal about burning down this tree house anyway?"

"I don't know. All I know is he has been acting very weird ever since that girl was murdered by the river."

"I know. I was dispatched to investigate the crime scene, but then he radioed in, telling me to stop, and said he would be doing the investigation himself. He instructed me to patrol the area, to be on the lookout for any suspects."

"Wow...that doesn't sound like him at all since he never does anything! He talks a lot about how he's over-worked, but I never see him do shit."

"Well, he must do something since the FBI got called in on that evidence-tampering thing."

"And he got re-elected. I mean, what do we see that everyone else doesn't?"

"The ladies sure trip over him. Even my wife likes him."

Both men looked up at the tree house. It almost felt like they could see me.

"So, what's the plan here?" Portly asked.

"The direct instructions from him are...we are to fill out an incident report stating that we were driving by on patrol when we observed a fire behind this house and what appeared to be a young boy running away into the woods."

"How young?"

Mullin shrugged. "The kid looks fifteen or sixteen. Then we call dispatch to have the fire department come out. Upon investigating the scene, we find gas cans and possible suspicious evidence from the tree house related to the murder of the Abby Meyer girl."

"What suspicious evidence?"

"No idea. He said he would take it from there."

Portly sighed. "The stupid things I have to do to get a promotion."

Mullin flipped open the cap on the yellow spout and began splashing the gasoline on the base of the tree.

CHAPTER 8

I had to think quick.

In the darkness, my hand searched for the folded note inside the Bible. I carefully slipped it out, then found the candle. I wrapped the paper around it. After striking a match and lighting the wick, I let go of the flaming candle and paper down through the opening in the floor.

Almost immediately, there was a fireball that flashed up...and I heard Officer Mullin scream.

Both officers scrambled back, throwing their gas cans out into the yard. A flame-trail followed each of the gas cans before exploding.

Mullin sprung back into the other officer, and they both fell to the ground when the gas ignited. Mullin's right boot and pant leg caught fire. Scooting himself across the grass, Mullin frantically patted the flames as best he could.

Not knowing what else to do, I reached for the Bible, grasping it in my hands up against my chest and bowed my head.

What came over me next was hard to explain...as I first felt a hot flash followed by a burst of energy throughout my body. It was more powerful than any adrenaline rush I'd experienced. It was like my body was being overtaken...or possessed.

Like a caged wild animal, I began spinning and smashing the Bible up against the walls of the tree house, growling and snorting like an enraged beast at the top of my lungs.

Then...I stopped.

I looked through the opening to see both of the wide-eyed officers running back to the squad car, speeding away as fast as possible.

The fire had fizzled out.

Drained, I collapsed in a heap on the floor.

I woke to feel a hand wiggling my leg.

I opened my eyes to see Mr. Kraus's head and arm poking up through the tree house floor, trying to wake me.

"Uh...hi," I said, confused.

"Good morning," he said as he pulled himself up through the opening in the floor. "Want to tell me what happened down there?"

Honestly, I didn't know what to say. And who would believe me?

I leaned against the tree house wall.

"Looks like a fire," Mr. Kraus said. "Possibly arson with the remnants of gas cans and all."

I opened my mouth to reply, but then faint voices and clicking noises came up from below. We both bent over to look down.

I could see three people walking around. An older woman dressed professionally pointing a wooden stick with a rubber tip directing two guys in black pants and white polo shirts. They both had cameras, snapping pictures and writing notes of the area surrounding the tree house.

It took a few seconds before I recognized the older woman—she was the one who had sat in the church pew behind me at Mr. Wendorf's funeral. She was strong looking, a large woman—not fat, just big. Very serious, hazel eyes, grayish hair.

"Do you know who she is?" I whispered.

"Rachel Connor. She called me, telling me we should see your father this morning. Come on, let's get going."

I let Mr. Kraus go down first, then I followed.

"Good morning, Rachel," Mr. Kraus said.

"Good morning." She looked a bit imperious.

She watched us as we hurried off to the truck parked next to two other vehicles.

As we pulled away, I could swear I saw her eyes sparkle and a slight smile touch her face.

While driving to the Walworth County Jail, Mr. Kraus handed me an envelope. Inside was the cash I had given him for the down payment of the house.

"You asked me why I didn't give Mr. Bennett the cash you gave me. He's a slick talker and a little slimy. He's also Judge Phillip Dru's realtor of choice. They work together, flipping houses. I've heard...well, negative stories about that. A check is much safer. A paper trail.

Cash can disappear. Bennett would rather sell high-priced lake property or houses in small towns than farm land or houses out in the countryside. People buying property out in the country take longer, doing surveys, checking mineral rights, liens, and easement searches, and things like that. Plus, people want to negotiate more because of it. Buyers in the small towns and around lakes are quicker to pay closer to the asking price."

"Well, Mr. Bennett wasn't very nice to me. I wanted to kick him in the...well, kick him. He made me so mad."

Mr. Kraus chuckled. "He does have an arrogance about him. He first asked for $10,000 down to hold the house, and when I agreed to pay the full $85,000 in cash, he said he had to make a phone call to somebody. I'm guessing it was either to your mother or Judge Dru in order to take a check for the $5,000 down payment."

"Did he say anything about her or where she is?"

He shook his head. "No."

"Well, if she wasn't home, then I wonder where he called her."

I thought about the bedroom at the Meyer Estate where I'd last seen her.

We walked up the steps into the county jail and followed the signs to the visitor area.

After signing in and talking to the male officer through a hole in a window, we took our seats.

A few minutes later, a metal door buzzed, and we were ushered into a secure room. Another door buzzed, and we were escorted by another officer to a small, plain conference room with two stools bolted to the floor. There was a counter facing a thick window, dividing us from the other side.

We waited.

Looking up, I noticed a security camera pointing down on us. Then the door on the other side buzzed and opened.

My father shuffled in wearing an orange short-sleeved prison jumpsuit, white plastic shower shoes, and a chain running up from his leg cuffs to the ones on his wrists. There was an officer on each side of him.

He smiled at me, but he looked pale, scared, unshaven, and his hair was not combed. The three of them just stood there for a moment, then I heard the door buzz again. The two officers escorted my father back out the door. And they were gone.

"What's going on?"

Mr. Kraus said, "I don't know."

Then our door buzzed loudly, and I jumped a little.

An officer walked in. "Mr. Corbett, the public defender representing Mr. Douglas, would not let his client speak to anyone without him being present. He said he won't be available today. I'm sorry, but you'll have to leave."

The officer turned and walked us out of the area.

Back in Mr. Kraus's pick-up truck, I asked:

"I wonder why Mr. Corbett wouldn't let us talk with Dad. Why couldn't he make it? I really wanted to talk to my father."

Mr. Kraus didn't answer.

As we drove by Mr. Wendorf's property, I saw the same two vehicles that had been parked in my driveway earlier now parked in Wendorf's driveway.

As we walked into the Kraus kitchen, Emma greeted us, saying she had beef stew simmering on the stove and freshly baked bread.

Mr. Kraus said, "Sounds good. We'll both have some. Load us up!"

Emma smiled. "I'll get it together after you wash your hands."

So, we did, then sat at the table and said our prayers before digging in. Once finished, Emma took away our dishes and wiped down the table.

"It was nice to see my father smile at me."

Mr. Kraus nodded. "Yes. But it was hard to see him so troubled."

"I hope Mr. Corbett is a good attorney. Do you know anything about him?"

"No, but I bet the Honorable Miss Connor knows about him."

"Who?"

"Rachel Connor, the lady you saw under the tree house this morning."

"How do you know her?"

"Small world, but Rachel is my wife's best friend and Mr. Wendorf's stepsister."

"But, you called her 'The Honorable.'"

"Rachel recently retired as a federal judge from the United States District Court for the Eastern District of Wisconsin. She was appointed in '72 if I remember correctly by then-President Nixon. Before that, she was highly respected and known as a fierce federal prosecutor for the same district."

Mrs. Kraus slowly entered the kitchen with her walker.

"Good morning," I said.

"Good morning, Dustin. Did you sleep okay?"

Lying a bit, I said, "Yes, thanks."

She sliced pieces of bread, pulled out a jar of what looked like strawberry jam from the refrigerator, then spread it on the fresh-cut slices.

Emma came over and helped her pass around slices to all of us.

Mrs. Kraus sat at the table besides Mr. Kraus as we nibbled on the bread.

Mr. Kraus pointed to me. "I was telling Dustin about Rachel."

She beamed brightly.

"Gosh, we grew up together and went to St. Gerard's Catholic school in Richmond. We also went on several mission trips around the world. I've always known Rachel to enjoy helping people, and she has been faithful to the Lord. During our last mission trip together, she seemed troubled and said she wanted to go to law school. I think she was torn because it...it wasn't considered the Lord's work."

She paused, momentarily gathering her thoughts, eyes looking around, re-focusing. "Rachel's mother, Betty, married Frances Wendorf—Ben Wendorf's father. This was a couple of years after Rachel's father, Joe, was tragically killed in a pen by a bull. 'Horned,' I believe the term is. Rachel had been in her first year at Moritz College of Law in Columbus, Ohio."

She paused, delicately taking a small bite of bread.

"Ben Wendorf's mother...Janet...well...as a young boy, maybe he was eight years old, Ben Wendorf broke his neck after a horse he was on got spooked, throwing him off. He hit his head hard on the ground, his boot got caught in the stirrup, and he got dragged off for over a mile. He suffered major brain trauma. It was horrific. He broke many other bones throughout his body and spent over four months in the hospital and had several surgeries in an attempt to restore his memory and repair his brain. The neurologist and doctors said he would never be normal.

"After the accident, Ben never did recognize his own mother. Janet mentally couldn't take it, and about six months later, one night, she just upped and left. Rumor has it, she ran off with a truck driver and has never been seen since."

"I had no idea that happened to Mr. Wendorf," I said.

"It was a long time ago. Ben walked with a limp after that. It was a couple of years after the accident that Betty—Rachel's mother—and Frances—Ben's father—married and moved to Texas. Ben was about ten or eleven, I would guess. Still in bad condition, but better."

Mr. Kraus sat back in his chair. "Ben Wendorf suffered from an anxiety disorder called *zoophobia*."

"Zoophobia?" I asked. "Afraid of zoos?"

Mr. Kraus chuckled. "You could say that. More accurately, he became fearful of animals. Horses in particular, but really anything on four legs. Sheep, cows, raccoons, goats. Most people didn't know that, so the stories became 'Old man Wendorf hates cats and dogs.'"

Emma, who had been out back hanging up the laundry, rushed in the door. "There is smoke rising up over the trees in the direction of the Douglas house."

Both Mr. Kraus and I scrambled to our feet and rushed out the door.

Emma was right. The smoke was coming from the area of my house. Mr. Kraus hurried back inside and called 9-1-1; then we got in the pickup.

CHAPTER 9

I wasn't prepared for the reality that my home was engulfed in flames! I sat staring through the windshield in total numbness as Mr. Kraus pulled to a stop on the side of the road.

The pleasant summer sky, with its calming blue and fluffy white clouds floating, collided against the backdrop of the dense black smoke rising, billowing into the atmosphere, orange-yellow flames curling up through the windows and roof. It looked like something from a Hollywood movie.

In the distance, the sound of sirens was growing closer.

As I got out to look at my tree house, a fire truck pulled to a halt, blocking my view of the backyard. I ran around it to see a smoldering tree trunk with branches that once held my little escape room burnt off. Everything else from the tree was gone.

I stopped and fell to my knees, staring at the burnt corpse of the tree, tears beginning to cloud my eyes into blurriness.

I felt a hand drop down on my shoulder.

"Oh, my dear Lord," Mr. Kraus said.

Then I heard someone race up. "Is he okay or need help?"

Mr. Kraus answered back: "No, he's okay."

Mr. Kraus helped me up. I buried my head into his chest and sobbed while he just held me.

After a couple of minutes, he said, "Let's go."

We slowly drove off back to the Kraus house. Other than the clothes I was wearing and my bike, I had lost everything.

Mrs. Kraus and Emma were seated at the kitchen table. Neither said a word as I walked past them toward the room I was staying in.

I collapsed onto the bed, feeling myself fall deeper and deeper into a calm blackness.

At some point, I fell into sleep.

I woke to the aroma of frying bacon. Though still devastated, I felt rested, and I accepted the fact that my tree house was now gone. There was nothing I could do about it anyway.

I lay looking around the room, filled with country crafts hanging on the walls, knickknacks sitting on shelves and atop the handmade dresser and nightstand. I noticed the window was open as the drapes slowly swayed with the breeze along with the sounds of distant birds chirping. I realized I had slept not just the rest of the afternoon but through the night.

A calmness fell over me. An odd kind of peace.

I went to the bathroom and took a shower. After getting dressed, I entered the kitchen with Emma standing over the stove.

She smiled. "Good morning, Dustin. Are you hungry?"

"Yes."

"How would you like your eggs cooked?"

"Over-easy."

A few minutes later, she slid the cooked eggs onto a plate along with a couple pieces of bacon and some buttered toast. She placed the plate in front of me, followed by a glass of milk and homemade jam out of the refrigerator.

I said, "Thank you," before plowing in and devouring the meal.

She chuckled. "You're welcome."

Emma sat down with her cup of coffee and opened *The Richmond Times*.

"Oh my...a young girl turned herself in yesterday morning to the authorities and confessed to shooting the Robert Schultz boy at the high school."

"Who?" I asked.

"Um...they didn't give her name because she's a juvenile. She claimed Robert was her boyfriend, and she wanted to break up with him to begin dating a boy named Rusty Appleby. She said in a statement she was afraid of Schultz but found the courage to tell him she no longer wanted to date him. That's when Schultz got extremely upset, telling her, 'I will kill Rusty.' During this time, he was waving a pistol."

I vaguely remembered Robert's girlfriend and vaguely recalled her name was Connie. "The girl was remorseful for killing Robert but was devastated when Rusty committed suicide. She turned herself in, no longer able to deal with the guilt. She also claimed Jimmie Becker was innocent as she said to have witnessed Jimmie help Rusty during a fight with Robert. After Jimmie wrestled the gun out of Robert's hand, the girl claimed to have seen Jimmie toss the weapon away. She claims that is when she picked up the gun and shot Robert. She then ran off with the gun and threw it off the bridge into the river."

"Wow," I said.

"Authorities are quoted as saying that divers found the gun in the river late yesterday evening, corroborating her story."

Emma laid down the paper. "The truth always bubbles to the surface. Sometimes it takes longer than we wish, but it always comes to light. She did the right thing by confessing. She may be imprisoned by the authorities, but she will not be held hostage to herself. She can be judged fairly by others."

"Good. Then someday the truth will bubble to the surface and be told of how my home and tree house caught fire."

"Yes," Emma said. "The truth will come to light."

I found Mr. Kraus by the barn hooking up a hay wagon to the hay-baler.

"Good morning, Dustin. Did you get some breakfast?"

"'Morning. Yes, Emma cooked me up some eggs."

"Are you ready to get started?"

"Sure. What's up for today?"

"I would like to get three wagons of hay baled and put up."

"Okay."

While riding out to the alfalfa field, the full morning sun was already getting hot and sticky, and as the day passed, it got even hotter as we worked through the midday. After eight hours of lifting and three wagons stacked with hay bales, I climbed down out of the stuffy loft covered in sweat and dust. My throbbing fingers stung inside the gloves from broken blisters after grabbing baling twine all day. It's hard to explain just how exhausted I felt from working so hard.

I entered the house while Mr. Kraus finished putting away the baler and tractor.

I immediately headed into the bathroom, stripped down, and turned the shower on cold. I stepped in and stood under the soothing water as it began to cool down my over-heated body. I watched the water with small pieces of hay swirl down the drain along with the dirt and dust washing off my skin. Slowly, the water turned clear.

The work helped my mind escape from dwelling on my current displaced life.

I got out of the shower, dried off, and stared at the dirty pile of clothes. I would need to buy new ones. For the moment, I had no choice; I re-dressed in what I had.

I walked into the kitchen and saw a frosted cake, burning candles, and three smiling faces. Mr. and Mrs. Kraus and Emma began singing "Happy Birthday!"

I was caught off guard. But it was June 5th, my sixteenth birthday, and I had forgotten all about it. I began to smile with my sun-dried face.

Mrs. Kraus said, "Make a wish and blow out the candles!"

"I think you all know what I will wish for...clean clothes!"

My real wish, of course, was to find the truth and discover what was going on and who was behind all the bad stuff of the last several days. But in one big breath, I blew out all the candles, hoping my wish would come true.

Emma began cutting the cake into slices. Chocolate with white buttercream frosting—my favorite!

Once we finished with the cake, Mr. Kraus slid a set of car keys across the table. "Happy Birthday!"

"What...what is this?" I said, surprised.

"Mrs. Kraus wants to give you a gift from all of us."

"Come, follow me," Mrs. Kraus said, smiling from ear to ear as Emma helped her stand and get her walker. "It's been years since I've taken a ride in this beautiful car."

We all followed Mrs. Kraus out the door to see.

"This is a 1967 Chevy Impala SS 427," Mr. Kraus said, "four-speed with original ermine white exterior and red vinyl interior."

It was sparkling and shining in the early evening sun. I couldn't believe I was being given such a generous gift. I was at a loss for words looking over this magnificent vehicle.

"I hope you like it, Dustin," Mrs. Kraus said. "And enjoy it just as much as my brother Michael did."

While Emma opened the front passenger door, assisting Mrs. Kraus inside, Mr. Kraus said, "Michael was Emily's younger brother, killed in the Vietnam War. He bought this car brand-new and drove it for a few months before he enlisted in the war. It only got a couple of thousand original miles before he parked it in the barn."

"This is what was under the tarp?" I asked.

Mr. Kraus beamed.

"Come on, Dustin—take us for a ride!" Mrs. Kraus said out the window.

Mr. Kraus and Emma crawled into the backseat as I climbed into the driver's seat and slid the key into the ignition. The engine cranked right up. My father had taught me how to drive his four-speed car, so I hoped it all came back. I was nervous, but I was ready to take it for a spin.

I put the car into first gear and slowly let the clutch out...and we were off!

"Turn left at the end of the driveway," Mrs. Kraus said.

After turning, I shifted into second, then third, and finally fourth as I sped up. I looked down at the speedometer—55 mph. Perfect!

"At the stop sign, turn left again."

I slowed for the stop, remembered to use the turn signal even though there was no one around, made the turn, and began shifting up through the gears again.

Mrs. Kraus pointed. "Turn into the church and go through the cemetery."

I pulled in and rolled around onto the gravel roadway behind the church, heading through the cemetery gate.

"The cemetery looks really nice," Mrs. Kraus said.

From the backseat, Mr. Kraus said, "Thanks."

After we wound our way through the cemetery, Mrs. Kraus asked me to pull over and stop. We all got out, Mr. Kraus and Emma helping Mrs. Kraus.

A couple rows in, we approached a headstone. I recalled my dad stopping at this one to share a story with me about a fine young man killed while serving our country in the Vietnam War. The military-style white headstone was inscribed *Army Private Michael J. Henson, July 9th, 1949 - February 12th, 1968, Vietnam War.*

Mrs. Kraus said softly. "Hi, Michael...it's been a long time."

Her hand rose to her cheek to wipe away a tear. She turned and looked to the headstone next to his.

Charles William Kraus was one name. *Emily Norma Kraus* was the other. It had dates of birth but nothing else. I realized this was the pre-inscribed headstone for the Kraus's.

"Oh, look!" Mrs. Kraus said, pointing at a deer about fifty yards away looking back at us. "Hi, Michael."

Emma whispered to me that just about every time she visited her brother's grave, she saw a deer nearby no matter what time of year it was. "In her mind, she believes it's a sign from her brother saying 'Hello.'"

Mrs. Kraus, holding Mr. Kraus's hand, said: "Soon we'll be together. Soon we'll all be together."

Mr. Kraus hugged and kissed her cheek ever so gently while she wept in his arms.

Emma and I stepped back to give them space.

Mrs. Kraus slowly looked up to Mr. Kraus. "Thank you for giving me such a wonderful life together. I've been so proud to be your wife. I love you, Bear!"

Mr. Kraus smiled with a twinkle in his eye. "I will never stop loving you, Scooter."

I laid in bed with heavy eyes, exhausted, but all I could do was think about the car gifted to me.

Mr. Kraus said in the morning we would go into town to shop for clothes, then he would go with me to get the car registered in my name, arrange car insurance, and go to take my road test.

I made a note to make a run with my bike to get some more money from the jars to help pay for everything.

I pulled the covers up over me as a chill slowly came up over me.

CHAPTER 10

The dream seemed so real...I suppose it was my mind's way of trying to understand some of what had been going on...

It opened finding myself standing in a thick, pink-purplish fog, looking around to figure out where I was. Outside, that was all I knew. I could feel grass under my bare feet. That was somewhat soothing, but the eerie stillness was kind of frightening.

I walked forward, and my leg bumped into something solid. I looked down to see a gravestone. I knelt down to get a closer view and saw writing etched into the white granite.

Michael Henson

Suddenly, something appeared in my peripheral vision, and I flinched, turning my head to see a dark figure approaching through the dense fog from behind the headstone.

It was my father dressed in a black suit, white shirt, and black tie. He was saying something, as if talking to himself.

I wanted to stand but couldn't. I kept still, studying him.

He was in mid-sentence:

"...he was brave taking on enemy fire. It was the bloodiest week of the war, during the Tet Offensive. Michael was just one of the 543 American soldiers who sacrificed their lives and died in Hanoi during that horrific battle."

His eyes turned down to the headstone, and he smiled when he saw me. "Hi, Dustin, I want to introduce you to..."

He looked around in the fog. "Where did he go? He was just here."

"I don't know," I said.

He looked back at me. "A lot has changed since I last saw you. Yes. A lot of things have changed." He paused. "Happy Belated Birthday! How do you like the Impala?"

I didn't know how to answer his question. I was puzzled how he even knew about the car. "It will be great for you," he said.

Then he looked away into the fog for a moment. He frowned. "Your mother is in really big trouble. You need to find her!"

Just after he said this, something like a lightning bolt illuminated the fog, followed by a sharp, loud crack.

My heart jumped, and then I froze in fear when a voice cut through the air...my mother's voice, far off.

"It's time for dinner!"

My father's expression was one of surprise.

And then in a blink, he vanished, along with the dream.

Still half-asleep, I sprung up in bed to a sitting position, my hands blindly batting the air as birds—yes, birds!— were attacking me from all sides.

Hot, with heart pounding hard, I became fully conscious, struggling to catch my breath.

3:12 am is what the clock read.

Laying back on the sweaty pillow, my eyes scanned the nothing of the darkness.

Trying to cool down, I threw the covers off me.

I went back through the dream.

My father had seemed relaxed until he heard my mother's voice. There was no mention of my mother's disappearance and odd behavior, other than that she needed help. He had said she was in "big trouble"—the same words she had used about him.

I had conflicted thoughts about my mother. I realized I didn't really know anything about her. She had always been mysterious and distant. And until now, I'd never questioned it. I'd thought that's just how women were. I mean, other than teachers or Mrs. Kraus—who until recently, I'd rarely interacted with—I just wasn't around females much at all.

I pulled the covers back up as thoughts about finding mother...suddenly felt dangerous.

After breakfast, Mr. Kraus and I headed to Richmond to go clothes shopping and get everything for the car done. I got seven shirts, two pairs of jeans, and several pairs of socks and underwear.

The time at the DMV for the registration and the road test took about an hour—I passed!—and the insurance only took fifteen or twenty minutes.

On our way back, I wanted to drive by my house...only, I didn't drive by—I pulled right into the driveway.

Mr. Kraus pointed. "Looks like Mr. Bennett has already been by to get his yard sign." He was right; it was gone.

As I got out of the car, surveying the charred rubble that once was my home and the burned-up tree that once held my tree house, a car pulled into the driveway. Two men got out. It was the same two guys who had been at the house the other morning as I'd watched from the tree house.

They both had cameras and notepads as they approached us.

"Hello," the shorter of the two men said.

"Good day," Mr. Kraus said. "May I ask what you are here for?"

"We are private investigators, here to investigate the cause of the fire." He pulled out and flipped open a wallet which showed a picture ID. I didn't read it, but Mr. Kraus leaned in to look.

"Do you have any idea who did it?" I asked.

"No, not yet."

"Who hired you guys?" Mr. Kraus asked.

"That's confidential," the taller man said; then they turned to walk toward the burnt area.

We got back in the Impala and drove back to the Kraus farm.

We found Mrs. Kraus, Emma, and Rachel Connor seated at the kitchen table.

Emma stood. "Are either of you hungry?

"I'm not," Mr. Kraus said.

Mrs. Kraus put her hand to her lips to clear her throat.

"Are you okay?" he asked.

"I had a tickle in my throat. Rachel has been sharing some not-so-good news she discovered this morning."

"Oh, really? What is it?"

Rachel hesitated for a moment.

"I went to the courthouse this morning to file some paperwork. That's when the clerk informed me Mr. Douglas..."

She glanced at me sadly.

"Mr. Douglas passed away late last night in his cell from a massive heart attack. He was rushed to the emergency room but was pronounced dead at the hospital. The first responders tried but couldn't bring him back."

It literally felt as though my heart fell into my stomach.

"NO! NO!" I shouted.

Mrs. Kraus struggled to stand without her walker. She stepped toward me and opened her arms as I fell into them.

"I'm sorry, Dustin."

Emma approached, and the two of them just held me while I stood in total emptiness.

Mr. Kraus and Rachel walked away into the living room to speak to each other.

In my head, all I could hear was...

It's time for dinner!

It's time for dinner!

It's time for dinner!

Emma and Mrs. Kraus guided me into a chair at the kitchen table. I laid my head onto the tabletop.

"My dad will never know the truth!" I said.

Emma's hand rested on my shoulder. "He already knows the truth."

"Yes," Mrs. Kraus said, "your father's spirit will help you understand and find the truth."

"I don't believe in silly miracles!"

There was a long pause. Then: "Maybe you should."

Emma's hand lightly rubbed my shoulder. "Miracles are hard to understand and believe. But if you really desire to discover the truth, sometimes miracles unexpectedly appear before you. They play an important role in uncovering what is real."

"Miracles come in different degrees," Mrs. Kraus said.

"How will I know when they happen?"

"You will."

Mr. Kraus and Rachel returned from the living room.

"I'm very sorry for your loss," Rachel said. "If you'll excuse me, I need to go." She then turned and continued out the door.

Mr. Kraus sat in a chair across from me.

"They found Mr. Wendorf's pickup truck abandoned in a bank parking lot in Frisco, Texas, just north of Dallas."

I lifted my head, thinking.

Is it possible Jimmie is on the run somewhere in Texas?

After a few minutes of awkward silence, Mr. Kraus added:

"We'll need to go to town in order to identify your father's body and make arrangements."

Though my tears eventually ran dry, the pain of losing my father still stung.

After standing in a room and having the sheet pulled back from the body, only then did it really become real. Dad was dead.

Mr. Kraus and I stopped at the diner to get something to eat and talk about Dad's final arrangements.

The waitress flopped down a couple of menus. "I'll be right back to take your order." The late afternoon diner was busy. Officer Mullin and his partner were seated at a booth not far away. I noticed Mullin couldn't take his nervous eyes off me. Soon, both officers got up and walked the long way around to avoid us before escaping out the door.

Over our meals, we discussed arrangements, and I decided to wait and have the formal services and burial at a later date.

When we went up to pay the bill, I saw the headline on *The Richmond Times*:

PASTOR DOUGLAS FOUND DEAD IN HIS CELL

Outside, we saw Mr. Thomas in a suit and tie, admiring my car.

As we approached, he looked up at Mr. Kraus. "Hi, Charles. Is this your car?"

"No, it's Dustin's car."

Turning his eyes to me, he smiled. "What a classic!" I nodded my head in agreement.

After some small talk about the car, Mr. Thomas said, "I am sorry to hear about your father."

"Thank you," I said.

"Charles, can I have a word?"

The two men walked off to the side of the diner's parking lot.

Driving to the funeral home in Richmond, not knowing Mr. Thomas, I asked Mr. Kraus to tell me more about him.

"Mr. Thomas is the president of Citizens National Bank in Richmond and is one of the original trustees of the Meyer Estate. He knew your father very well. Mr. Thomas worked long hours together with your father and the attorneys to establish the Meyer Foundation. I told him your thoughts on your father's service being held at later date, and he agreed, saying, 'That would be best.'"

I thought about the kind words Mr. Thomas had shared about Mr. Wendorf at his service. Feeling a little inquisitive, I asked, "Mr. Thomas said he knew Mr. Wendorf as a young boy. How did he know him?"

"They grew up as neighbors, played, and went to school together. Mr. Thomas has said many times that after that horrific horse accident involving Ben, he never recognized or remembered him and was never the same." I sat listening as Mr. Kraus continued. "Mental illness is very hard for most people to understand. But Mr. Thomas understood and remained a loyal friend throughout the years, despite what took place to him. Once Ben turned eighteen, he moved back to Wisconsin from Texas. Mr. Thomas was given authority and oversaw Ben's finances and paid his bills on his behalf out of an annuity account set up by Ben's father many years ago for the long-term care of him and his great-grandmother's property he lived on."

We arrived at the funeral home, parked, and went inside.

The cost of getting my car registered, insured, and the pre-arrangements for my father took all the cash I had. I still needed to pay the funeral home a balance of $800. I got it all done thanks to Mr. Kraus's guidance.

After returning to the Kraus farm, I felt restless. I wanted to take my bike out for a ride before dark—something familiar. So, with the warm sun slowly dipping into the western sky, I headed through the woods, going to the first oak tree with the jars buried under it from Jimmie's map. After sliding the stone over and scratching away the dirt...

...the jars were gone.

Looking around, I knew it had to be the right tree.

I took off for the second spot to see if those jars and plastic containers were still buried there. Again...nothing!

Baffled, I pedaled toward the third location—the flat rock by the oak tree on the far back corner of Mr. Wendorf's property. Before I got there, I slammed on the brakes.

Off in the distance, over the rusty old tractor and plow, held within the oak tree branches was a...tree house!

I stared in disbelief. It wasn't just a tree house, but *my* tree house.

I approached, breathless. I stood looking up the boards, going up to the opening.

I said out loud: "I didn't believe in miracles."

I crawled up through the opening.

The sun was filtered through the stained-glass window, emitting colorful light. It was surreal but calming.

I scooted myself across the floor and saw a piece of paper sticking out the side of the Bible, just like before. It was in the same beautiful cursive handwriting as the other note.

Please find me!

I set it down and looked up to see I was immersed in a pinkish-purple hazy glow. I glanced to the stained-glass window. The purple cross my father had set into the center was radiating.

Then I heard something milling around under the tree house.

Looking down through the opening in the floor, standing by the old tractor was a deer. It was staring up at me. It was as if our eyes locked on each other momentarily before it bounced away. Rubbing my eyes, I sat back up...and the purplish glow was gone.

I looked back down to the note...

Please find me!

CHAPTER 11

The house was quiet when I entered. Both Mr. and Mrs. Kraus were in their bedroom for the night. A sliver of light peeked out from under the door, and I could hear muffled conversation.

I went to my room, closed the door softly, and turned on the light. I sat on the edge of the bed, trying to figure out who had wrote the "Please find me" note.

Find who? Jimmie?

From the hallway, I heard a squeaking, followed by a shuffling sound. A faint knock and a soft voice: "Dustin...are you awake?"

I stood up, moving to the door. "Yes," I said as I opened the door.

Mrs. Kraus was hunched over in her robe, holding onto her walker.

I helped her to the wooden rocking chair by the window. I sat back on the edge of the bed.

"This rocking chair brings back a lot of memories," she said. "My father built it by hand many, many years ago. For my mother. A lot of time has gone by since then."

She paused, looking wistful. I still wasn't sure why she wanted to see me.

"As a child, we grew up with dirt floors. At the time, I thought that was normal. The warmth and love my parents gave us seemed endless and overshadowed the rough times. Those feelings are still alive inside me today."

She looked around.

"This room is filled with memories of my life."

I smiled, and she smiled back. Then she pointed.

"I watched my father teach my brother Michael how to construct that nightstand, the dresser, and the bed. Sometime, you should look under the bed. You'll find a homemade case with a well-worn wooden train set inside. My grandfather—on my father's side of the family—whittled it for my father to play with when he was six or seven years old. Dad said he played with it for years.

"My mother shared the story about her family, who fell on such hard times that her mom and dad would make handmade toys out of wood and old clothes. Then they would wrap them up to give as gifts for birthdays and Christmas. I still have the handmade dolls and a dollhouse set up in our bedroom. Together, my grandfather and grandmother crafted those."

Her voice was dreamy, soft, and soothing.

"My mother loved to rock in this chair, crocheting or mending an old shirt. After dinner, my father would sit on a small bench by her side and tell stories about his day."

"Yeah," I said. "I miss my father telling stories about his day at the dinner table."

"I think you've found life can be both hard to understand and humbling at the same time."

A brief pause.

"Dustin, life is a journey through humility and challenges. You have to find the strength to hold on to hope."

Looking down, I nodded my head in agreement.

"I remember the day like it was yesterday, July 28th. My father's 96th birthday. I stopped over to visit my parents and wish him a happy birthday. I found my mother napping in this rocking chair."

She paused again.

"Only, she wasn't sleeping. When I went to wake her...well, she had passed away. In her hands were a pair of pants she was mending. That was the only time I ever saw my father cry."

Her eyes filled up with old memories.

"My father once said to me, 'During troubled times, we can easily fail to accept or see the good around us.' Our minds can become clouded and consumed with uncontrollable ill thoughts. That's when you know you're being challenged by moral choices. And if you're not careful, you can be lured into dark places.'"

She sighed.

"Many people never return and become tools of evil."

"Evil?"

"Yes. Evil exists in the dark unknown and preys on one's passions, lack of self-esteem, or vulnerabilities."

I frowned. "Do you think my mother is evil?"

"I don't really know your mother, so it's hard to honestly say. But something may have nibbled its way into her soul."

I considered this, then decided to change the subject.

"Tell me about the different miracles."

"May I ask why?"

"I think I may have experienced one today."

"Did you? Tell me what happened."

"Somehow my tree house reappeared in the oak on Mr. Wendorf's property. And once I was up in it, a purplish-pink haze came over me. Then when I looked out the opening, a deer appeared, staring up at me."

Mrs. Kraus didn't say anything.

"Do you believe me?"

"Yes. Most people wouldn't believe you telling them, but I do. Miracles are unexpected gifts."

She paused again, frowning.

"I am sorry, but Rachel shared with me after you and Charles left earlier today that...well, she had your tree house disassembled before the fire happened, then reconstructed up in the tree on Mr. Wendorf's property. She said she'd felt something bad was going to happen—and, it did!"

"How did she know?"

"She just...felt it. I don't know. Something was not right."

After saying goodnight, Mrs. Kraus turned in for the evening, and I lay curious and restless. Then I got up and pulled the wooden case out from under the bed. Once open, I sat in awe, staring at the fine detail whittled into each piece of the handmade train. I lifted open a little door alongside the train pieces and found the wooden track.

Mrs. Kraus was right. They were well-worn. Her father must have played with this train set for countless hours as a child.

I placed the track pieces on the floor in an oval shape. Then I carefully put each piece of the train, starting with the engine, followed with six different types of box and coal cars on the track. Last, I hooked up the caboose.

It was fascinating to watch each wheel of the train turn in circles, being guided by the track.

I played with it for hours into the night.

That brought to me the greatest memory I cherished the most: helping my father build the tree house.

When I awoke, I discovered I had fallen asleep on the floor next to the train set.

I sat up, gently placing each piece back into its rightful spot in the case, then I re-slid the case back under the bed.

Then I left the room, went outside, got on my bike, and headed for the tree house.

Rachel said it...something isn't right!

I climbed up through the bottom opening.

The piece of paper was lying on the floor.

Please find me!

A million thoughts seemed to run through my mind.

I sat back and took a big breath, trying to calm my nerves.

Looking over the inside of the tree house, I could see it was perfectly reconstructed.

On the wall inside, I found the two bullet casings nailed into the bark.

It was almost as if the tree house had not only been moved...but the whole tree!

I considered Jimmie's motivation...what was he trying to tell me?

He'd been missing since Robert was shot and killed.

I had a sneaking suspicion that Jimmie might have had something to do with Mr. Wendorf's pickup truck being found in Texas.

And then I'd discovered the jars were missing at two of the locations— places on his map he'd left for Abby to give me.

I bent over to look down at the ground by the base of the tree, wondering about the third location...and what, if anything, was buried under it.

I heard car doors slam shut.

I peeked through the boards, seeing the two investigators standing by their vehicle. Then, they walked toward the dilapidated tool shed next to Mr. Wendorf's overgrown garden and disappeared inside.

My nose was pressed against the boards, my eyes studying what I could see around the old shed.

The two men reappeared with a third person. They quietly guided a hooded figure. The third seemed weakened and struggled to walk. They placed the person into the back seat of the car. I noticed their hands had been bound behind their back.

The two men got in the car and drove off.

I sat back against the wall, and the pinkish-purple haze reappeared throughout the inside of the tree house. It was calming as it started to gather into a beam of purple light that seemed to be drawing itself out through the purple cross in the window.

And just as fast as it appeared, it was gone.

I went down the tree and found the boards stacked along the side of the tool shed had been moved and re-stacked. The first set of doors were open, allowing clear access to the storm cellar door.

I stepped down the concrete stairs and slowly opened the door. Immediately, I could smell what seemed like heavy perspiration coming from above.

Stepping in, I saw all the jars, plastic containers, and wooden shelving were gone. In the middle of the small room was a wooden chair. Rope hung down from hooks screwed into the parallel beams of timber that ran along the ceiling.

Another chair was behind the small drop-leaf table which acted like a desk along the wall.

I physically jolted when I saw someone looking at me! It turned out to be a reflection in a floor-to-ceiling mirror.

Behind the mirror, I saw another chair.

I realized it was a two-way mirror.

In the dimly lit corner next to it, I saw four floodlights atop a tripod pointing at the chair. I flipped on the switch, and the room was blinded from the intense lights. I could feel the heat from them.

The chair placed behind the mirror sat in darkness.

The lights illuminated the floor and chair, and I could see droplets of blood.

I quickly flicked off the light and hurried out the cellar, slamming the door behind me.

Back up in the tree house, I grabbed the Bible off the shelf and opened it.

Bless this little tree house.

Off in the distance, I heard a tractor approaching.

I replaced the Bible on its shelf and climbed down. It was Mr. Kraus on his tractor out in one of his fields that was next to Mr. Wendorf's property.

He saw me and waved. Then he shut off the tractor and walked over to the barbed wire fence.

"I went in to check on you this morning, but you were gone."

"Yeah, after Mrs. Kraus told me last night that Rachel had my tree house reconstructed over here, I wanted to come check it out."

"How did it turn out?"

"Everything is exactly as it was. It's amazing. I wonder why she did it?"

"You'll have to ask her next time you see her. In the meantime, can you help me out?"

"Sure!"

So, I assisted Mr. Kraus bale and put up three wagons of hay.

After work and a cool shower, I jumped in the car and headed out. I parked it just off the road, not far from the Meyer Estate.

Sneaking through the woods, I hesitated once I saw the buildings through the trees. Then a sheriff's vehicle rolled up into the driveway. It parked in front of the brick four-car garage.

I crept in closer to get a better look.

A male officer got out of the car and stood with his back to me.

"It's time for dinner!"

My mother's voice...from somewhere nearby.

The officer turned toward the house, revealing his face. He was the same man I had seen in bed with my mother.

And he wasn't just an officer...he's the sheriff!

CHAPTER 12

I was in the Kraus's driveway when I saw Emma walking toward her house for the evening. She saw me and stopped.

"There's a plate of spaghetti and meatballs in the refrigerator for you. Have a nice night." Even though it sounded good, for some reason, I wasn't hungry. I went through the kitchen door and found Mrs. Kraus seated at the kitchen table with Rachel.

"Hi Dustin. Emma put together a dinner plate for you," Mrs. Kraus said.

"Great, thanks," I said. I turned to Rachel. "Mrs. Kraus told me you felt the importance to relocate my tree house. Can I ask why?"

"Yes, I did that."

I noticed she didn't answer my question.

"But I thought it burnt down in the fire."

She offered a small smile. "Hopefully you're not the only one who thought that."

"May I ask what's going on?"

"You can ask, but I don't have any answers right now."

I paused, trying to think through this confusion. She knew but she wouldn't tell me? Why?

"When I first saw the tree house at Wendorf's, I have to admit, I thought I had experienced a miracle."

"From what I understand," Mrs. Kraus said, "you did experience a miracle once up inside the tree house."

I stood, saying nothing. I needed to know more, but at the moment, I was speechless. It was probably from my exhaustion.

Both Rachel and Mrs. Kraus looked at me with concerned expressions.

I tried to make them feel better. "I'm thankful you had my tree house moved."

"You're welcome, Dustin," Rachel said. "I am sorry for being so vague with you, but when I find out anything I can share, when the time is right, I promise, I will tell you."

I nodded. "Is Mr. Kraus still up?"

"No," Mrs. Kraus said. "He said he was tired and turned in early."

"Okay," I said. "I think I'll do the same. Good night."

Rachel said, "Dustin—in time, the truth will be spoken."

The next morning, Emma was in the laundry room folding clothes next to the kitchen. "Morning, Emma. Have you seen Mr. Kraus?"

"Yes. He is mowing the cemetery this morning. He also said he had a burial today too. Are you hungry?"

"No."

"You need to eat something," she said as I went out the door.

At the cemetery, I found Mr. Kraus on a riding mower. When he spun around to take another pass, he saw me getting out of my car. With the mower deck raised and the blades off, he steered my way.

"Morning, Dustin."

"Morning."

"Are you okay?"

"No."

"What's wrong?"

"A lot! I found her."

"Who?"

"My mother."

"Where did you find her?"

"At the Meyer Estate. I think she's up to something with the sheriff."

"The sheriff?"

"Yes. I will never forget his face!"

"Why do you think it was him?"

I told him what I saw, about hearing my mother's voice, and the man turning so I could see his face.

"Are you sure it was the sheriff?"

"Yes. I'm positive."

I told him how I'd seen my mother being intimate with the sheriff.

When I was finished, there was a sound, and we looked over to see a funeral procession rolling in through the cemetery gate. The hearse stopped by a gravesite covered with a pop-up tent.

"Al Bennett's mother, Katherine, passed away. So, I'm sure Al will be in attendance."

Watching everyone exit their vehicles, I pointed. "There he is."

He was the only one wearing dark glasses, and he seemed to be walking with a slight limp.

Mr. Kraus said, "Come on, I want to show you something."

We walked over to the top of a knoll that overlooked the entire cemetery. Mr. Kraus paused, looking back and forth across the cemetery grounds. "This is my favorite spot in the cemetery."

It was easy to see why. With the church silhouetted in the background, all was peaceful.

It was like we were shepherds watching over the entire cemetery.

"I studied the plot map of the cemetery," Mr. Kraus said, "and there are four spaces available right here." He pointed down the slope. "I would recommend that spot to bury your father."

Then he pointed across the cemetery.

"Emily, Michael, and myself will be buried right over there. Maybe someday you and your wife can be buried next to your father. And someday, we'll all be together again.

We headed down the knoll toward the graveside service.

As we approached, I saw Al Bennett was sitting alone by the flowered casket under the tented area. Everyone else was gone. Once he saw us, he gathered himself.

"I'm sorry about the loss of your mother," Mr. Kraus said to Mr. Bennett.

"Thank you, Charles...I am going to miss her." Al's voice cracked a little.

After a few moments of silence, Mr. Kraus asked: "Any word on what took place at the Douglas house?"

Shifting from foot to foot, Al was clearly uncomfortable with the question.

"No...all I've heard is it's still under investigation. Good thing the bank placed a hold on your check."

"No, actually I did that!" Mr. Kraus said.

Turning quickly, Al said, "I better be going."

He limped off toward his car.

Then Al suddenly stopped, turned around, and snarled back to us: "I swear I don't know anything about the 'girls'!" Then he continued on to his car.

"What was that all about?" I asked. "Girls?"

"I don't know. But he looks like he was on the losing end of something."

"And he sure didn't want to talk about the fire at my house."

"No, he sure didn't."

"Did you notice his swollen eyes? That they were all black and blue?"

"And the bandage on his cheek," Mr. Kraus said.

Then it occurred to me: Al Bennett had the same limp as the hooded figure I had seen at the Wendorf farm when the two investigators were escorting someone out of the old tool shed.

After leaving the cemetery, I drove past the Meyer Estate. I didn't see anything unusual, but the thought of knowing my mother was there really creeped me out. And it made me pause. I needed more answers.

My stomach growled with hunger, so I drove back to the Kraus's.

Emma warmed up the leftover spaghetti and meatballs, and within minutes, it was gone. While eating, something else came to mind. I needed to know what was under the flat rock beneath the tree house.

At Wendorf's, I slid the flat rock aside. I saw the top of a jar. Wiping away the dirt, I pulled it out.

Inside was money and a folded note.

I unscrewed the lid and pulled out the note.

Meet me here at midnight on Saturday.

Jimmie's handwriting.

I paused. Things had been so crazy, I wasn't even sure what day of the week it was.

That had been happening way too often.

I heard car doors slam shut.

I peeked up from behind the tractor to see another hooded figure being escorted toward the old tool shed.

I stuffed the note into my front pocket, reburied the jar, and pedaled off.

"Emma, what day of the week is it?"

"Saturday." A long pause. "Is everything okay?"

"Yes. I lost track of...stuff, that's all."

"I guess summer break can do that to you."

I saw Mr. Kraus's pickup pulling into the driveway, parking by the barn.

"Hey, Dustin," he said when he saw me approaching. "What an interesting day."

"Why do you say that?"

"A couple of hours after you left the cemetery, a sheriff's deputy pulled in to ask me when the last time I saw Officer Mullin was."

"Why?"

"Apparently, he went missing. Supposedly, he was last seen at the diner eating lunch. Then they found his squad car abandoned, pulled just off the road next to a field about two miles away."

I lay in bed, wide-awake, watching the blue numbers on the clock. When it changed to 11:30 pm, I rolled out of bed, got dressed, and quietly slid open the window before sneaking out. It was a still, moonless night, so I had to be extra careful winding myself through the woods toward the tree house.

When I got there, I pulled a candle out of my pocket and lit it. I looked in between the boards of the old tool shed.

Nothing. It was pitch black. I went up into the tree house.

I pulled out the note left inside the Bible.

Please find me!

If it was my mother, I'd found her. In that dream, my father had said: "Your mother's in big trouble...you need to find her."

She didn't *seem* to be in big trouble or need help. Maybe it's the kind of trouble I didn't understand yet.

A shiver rolled over me. How she'd just taken off, not caring about me or my birthday.

I heard a rustling noise.

"Dustin, are you up there?"

Jimmie's voice!

I re-slid the note back into the Bible.

Jimmie's head popped up, and I felt relief and happiness at seeing his face.

After some small talk, our backs up against the walls, Jimmie asked, "What did the paper say about Robert?"

"Connie confessed to shooting Robert."

He nodded. "I picked up the bullet casing after she shot him and ran off to the tree house. I pounded it into the bark. I wanted you to know that I knew the truth!"

I pointed to the two bullet casings nailed into the bark.

Jimmie's eyes filled with surprise. "How did they get here?"

"Rachel had my tree house relocated here before the fire at my house."

"Who's Rachel? And why did she move the tree house here?" Jimmie asked.

"Rachel is Mr. Wendorf's stepsister. She is also a retired federal judge and Mrs. Kraus's best friend from childhood. I don't know who or how they moved the tree house here. Or why this place was chosen. Rachel said 'something wasn't right,' and that's why she had it moved."

"Whoever relocated it did a great job."

"I know. My father would be proud."

"How's your dad doing?"

I paused. "He's dead."

"Dead?"

I filled him in on what had happened to my father.

"Wow. I am so sorry," he said.

"So much has taken place since you left, sometimes it's hard to think straight."

"I know the feeling."

We talked in detail about what had happened to each of us, trying to piece everything together.

"I don't believe your father would hurt Abby," Jimmie said. "Just before I took off for Texas, she gave me a note. It said she was going to go into hiding...if they didn't find her first."

Jimmie showed me the note.

It was written in the same fancy cursive handwriting as the other notes I found in the tree house.

I reached for the Bible and opened it to where the note was inside. I showed Jimmie. "That is Abby's handwriting. I'm sure of it!"

From below, headlights swept across Mr. Wendorf's driveway as a car pulled in. Doors opened and slammed shut.

I blew out the candle.

We were surrounded by darkness as we stared out in between the boards.

CHAPTER 13

We couldn't see a thing.

Then we heard the car doors slam shut again. I could see taillights as the vehicle rolled away, out the driveway, headlights off.

Jimmie asked. "What is going on here?"

I re-lit the candle. "I don't know. All I know is all the money you left under the oak trees and under the old tool shed is missing."

"What? It's all missing?"

"All gone! Except for the jar beneath this tree."

Jimmie looked perplexed. "What did you do with the map?"

I had to think what I did. I rubbed my forehead, trying to remember. Then it came back to me.

"I had it in my front pants pocket. But that was when I changed jeans before the fire."

"The fire? You mean Wendorf's?"

"No—my house burned down!"

"What!"

"My father was arrested, and my mother put the house up for sale. Then the house caught fire and was destroyed."

"Do you think your mother found the note before the fire and took the money?" I bit my lip, shaking my head, thinking about all the possibilities. "I don't know." Jimmie stared at the note I had found in the Bible.

I pointed at it. "Do you think Abby is still alive?"

"Yes. This kind of proves it."

"It doesn't make any sense. What about the crime scene and the blood the police found by the river?"

"I know...it doesn't make any sense. Maybe it wasn't her."

"So, if you think Abby is still alive, why would my dad be accused of killing her? I don't understand any of this. Where do you think she is?" I asked.

"I don't know. But that's why I came back—to find her."

"You don't think Abby would have taken the money?" I asked.

He shook his head. "I doubt it. I mean, I got a sense that she was good, you know? Honest. There's just so much we don't know."

I sighed.

Rachel was right. Something was very wrong.

Jimmie tapped the note. "You said all the money is missing from the storm cellar under the old tool shed."

"Yes."

"What's down there now?" Jimmie asked.

"When I first went down there, I saw jars and containers stacked from floor to ceiling with money. Then, when I went back the second time, that was all gone. Instead, there was a single chair placed in the middle, with ropes hanging down over it. And there were spotlights and one of those two-way mirrors in a corner with a chair hidden behind it."

"That sounds creepy."

"Yeah, and I also found drops of blood on the chair and floor around it."

"Blood?"

"Weirder is that I've also seen someone hooded and bound being escorted in and out of the old shed."

"Hooded? Who was escorting them?"

"I think they were the private investigators."

"How do you know they are private investigators?"

"That's what they told me and Mr. Kraus."

"Where did they tell you that?"

"At my house, after the fire."

"Are you sure they were the same two investigators?"

"I'm not a hundred percent sure. They were too far away. But they dressed the same and drove the same kind of car. I think one of the hooded people might have been Al Bennett, the realtor."

"Why?"

"Because when I saw Mr. Bennett at his mother's service earlier this morning, he acted really weird and had a limp similar to the first hooded figure."

"Where do you think your mother is?" Jimmie asked.

"The Meyer Estate. I saw her there with the sheriff."

"Sheriff Lewis? How do you know he is the sheriff?"

"I recently saw a picture of the sheriff in the newspaper. A face I will never forget. Something is going on between them."

"What do you mean?"

I shook my head. "I'm going to leave it at that." I paused. "Can I ask you a question? Why did you leave without saying a word?"

Jimmie looked very sad.

"After Mr. Wendorf shot himself, I found a sealed envelope lying on the end table next to him. It had a note on it saying to take the sealed envelope to an attorney's office upon his death. The address was in Texas. So, that's what I did."

"What was in the envelope?"

"The attorney opened it and said it was his living trust."

"Is that like a will?"

Jimmie shrugged. "I guess so. Since I was the one who turned it in, I am a beneficiary of his estate."

"Seriously?"

I began to hear the pitter-patter of raindrops on the roof.

"The attorney knew the whole story—and boy, does he like to talk. Anyway, Mr. Wendorf's great grandfather—Eddie Wendorf—set up the living trust a long time ago. He was considered to be a wildcatter."

"What's a wildcatter?" I asked.

"Well…let me tell you the whole story, according to the attorney. Eddie's mother Edith—a widow—brought her son to America from Europe in the late eighteenth century after his father died from fever when Eddie was seven years old.

"Their ancestors originated from France in the twelfth century before having to escape religious persecution to a small village, Scramberg, located in the western territory of Württemberg, Germany. It's in the Black Forest, and it was there that his family changed their last name from Montagut to Wendorf.

"After entering through Ellis Island, both Edith and Eddie settled in Milwaukee with Edith's brother's family. Being young, adventurous, and needing money, Eddie worked endless hours with his uncle at a metal machine shop that custom built parts for ships.

"When Eddie was fourteen, he took off south to the Pineywoods of eastern Texas, where he worked as a lumberjack harvesting pine trees. Just before he left for Texas, his mother gave him an ancient cross. It had been secretly handed down through his father's side of the family for centuries. Legend has it that the old iron cross dates back to the Templars from France. The cross was meant to keep Eddie safe and bring him prosperity."

"Did it?" I asked.

"Yes. And from what the attorney told me, the cross also brought him great fortune. Upon his mother's death, Eddie returned to Wisconsin to fulfill his mother's final wishes. He secretly placed the cross under her headstone to bring her eternal life."

"That's very interesting," I said. "Through the years, my dad would tell me stories about the Templars. I wonder if he knew anything about this cross?"

Jimmie shrugged his shoulders.

"I guess we'll never know," I said.

"I guess not. Eddie worked hard and saved up every penny he could, and when he was seventeen, he bought his first hundred-acre tract of land in Texas. He also bought three Lincoln Red beef cows."

"I've never heard of them."

"From what I was told, the breed originated in Lincolnshire. In England. They have the ability to thrive under drought conditions, so they were ideal for the climate in eastern Texas. Anyway, that's when Eddie became a wildcatter, discovering oil on his land by drilling. And, over time, he ended up acquiring 746 acres of land just south of Tyler, Texas. He purchased another 24 acres by Decatur, Texas."

"I never knew any of this about Mr. Wendorf's family," I said.

Jimmie nodded. "Eddie and his wife are buried on their big Somerset Ranch, along with their son Jack and his wife Betty. Jack's son—Frances—is Mr. Wendorf's father."

"It sounds like that attorney knew everything about the Wendorf's."

Jimmie nodded. "He was intrigued by all this, like a history professor, and he spent hours explaining everything to me. Everything. For example, there are five pump-jacks on this property in eastern Texas and two more on the property outside of Decatur."

"Pump-jacks?" I asked.

"It's a rig that pumps oil out of the ground. And they're still pumping oil today. At some point, Eddie purchased this fifteen-acre farm here in Wisconsin. And the attorney said the mother, Edith, is buried somewhere here on this property, supposedly under an oak tree."

We sat for a while, listening to the rain, and I eventually closed my eyes and drifted off to sleep, falling into a dream.

In the dream, I found myself walking in a familiar purplish haze toward the tree house. Except the tree house wasn't there.

This seemed to be a time much earlier, back when the tractor was shiny and new, and a younger Mr. Wendorf sat behind the wheel under the oak tree.

Then I saw my father approach Mr. Wendorf as he climbed down off the tractor. My dad looked so much younger.

"Hi, Ben."

Mr. Wendorf looked at him but didn't say anything.

"Is this the oak tree that your father's great-grandmother is buried under?"

"Yes, and now it's time to leave this tractor to rest in peace. It's getting too difficult to mow her grave. I remember my father would mow here when I was a young boy. So, I've continued to mow it every week during the spring, summer, and fall."

Mr. Wendorf paused, looking wistful.

"This is the only place all the buzzing noise inside my head stops... even if it's just temporary. I've never understood why it helps my mind escape all the pain, the voices and fear that reside inside me. This is the only place that makes me feel calm and safe. It's magical here."

He paused again, this time frowning.

"To remember the young boy so alive, dreaming about the endless possibilities. This was before the darkness entered my life. That tragic day of my accident. A darkness at times. A darkness I fear and don't understand. With the tractor parked here, maybe someday...somebody will discover this tranquil place and find their purpose in life."

The purple haze became thick, to the point I could see nothing, and I stood frozen, not knowing where to go or what to do.

Then the haze receded a little.

My father—now older again—began walking, spreading something from his hand like some kind of black dust, particles, falling and floating down to the ground under the oak tree.

He saw me and stopped to lean up against the old rusty tractor surrounded by overgrown weeds and tall grass.

"Hi, Dustin."

"What are you doing?" I asked.

"Mr. Wendorf wanted to be buried here. But since his body was turned into ashes by the fire, I wanted to spread his ashes here."

The purple haze grew thick again and all disappeared. An eerie roar came over me for a few moments.

And then it faded away as the purple haze became thin again.

I could see my father standing on the knoll in the cemetery, in the same spot Mr. Kraus and I had stood.

"This would be a wonderful spot to be buried. Right here."

"Yes," I said. Then I asked: "Is Abby still alive?"

He nodded. "Yes, she's still alive."

"I saw Mother at the Meyer Estate," I said.

"She's in big trouble, Dustin. You need to ask her about the girls."

The dream ended.

CHAPTER 14

I woke with a chill; the damp, cool air made me rub my legs and arms to warm them. I didn't know when Jimmie left or where he went, but I was alone in the tree house.

I sat up to light the candle when I heard rustling coming from down below.

I poked my head over the edge to look down and heard grunting, heavy breathing and what sounded like slapping. I could barely make out two figures wrestling on the ground, punching each other.

One figure was much bigger and looked like he had the upper hand. An arm reared back before he swiftly landed a devastating blow to the head of the smaller figure—who seemed to have been knocked out and lay lifeless on the ground.

"That will teach you...you little bastard!"

The man was out of breath, but I thought I recognized the voice.

It took a few moments to come to me.

The sheriff!

I realized the sheriff had handcuffed the unconscious person, then placed a hood over their head. Then he bent down, grabbed the person by the collar, and dragged them off into the woods.

I was stunned and not sure what to do. He had just kidnapped Jimmie!

I should try to rescue him, but the sheriff was not just big but had a gun. And I figured if he was going to kill Jimmie, he would have done it already.

What do I do? What do I do?

"Oh my God..." I said as I raced into the kitchen. "...he took him!"

Emma spun around from the stove, wielding a spatula, startled at my entrance. Mr. Kraus was at the kitchen table, a cup of coffee in front of him.

"Who took who?" he asked.

"The sheriff...Jimmie...my friend Jimmie!"

"Okay, okay. Take a breath."

"The sheriff...the sheriff kidnapped Jimmie!"

"Dustin, please, take a moment to calm down," Mr. Kraus said as Mrs. Kraus came scooting into the kitchen.

I worked at catching my breath and gathering my thoughts...when I realized...

"The sheriff was coming for me...not Jimmie!...He must have thought... Jimmie was me!"

Emma set down the spatula and gently touched my arm. "Sit down and tell us what happened."

Mrs. Kraus called Rachel after I went through everything, and she came over with one of the private investigators.

I was uneasy at his presence since I wasn't sure who I could trust outside of the Kraus's. I wasn't even sure about Rachel Connor.

They took a seat at the table, and the man's eyes locked with mine for a moment before he nodded once and looked down at the notepad in front of him, writing something.

Emma placed cups of coffee in front of them, and Rachel gave me a slight smile. "Dustin, I would like to introduce David Zundel. He is a US Federal Marshall." She paused, letting that sink in.

"I thought you said you were a private investigator," I said.

He nodded. "That was a cover story. Sometimes when we say we're with the feds, people get upset."

"Yes," Rachel said. "There has been an investigation going on, and there are some things we cannot really discuss or talk about." She took a sip of her coffee. "I would like you to take your time and help us out with some questions we have."

She looked at the Kraus's and Emma, nodding slightly.

The three of them filed out of the kitchen.

"Tell me what you know about Officer Mullin," the Marshall said.

I did, and they both asked more detailed questions. I answered as best I could. It took about an hour as they asked different things about different people, Zundel taking three or four pages of notes.

They both stood, and Zundel said, "We'll find your friend." He then stuck out his hand to shake. "You've been a big help."

After they left, Mr. Kraus cocked his head toward the door.

"Let's go for a ride."

We drove through the fields to the back of Mr. Wendorf's property. Once at the fence line, we got out, hopped through the barbed wire fence, then headed toward the tree house.

Mr. Kraus paused at the base. "Show me which direction the sheriff dragged your friend off into the woods."

I pointed to a spot several yards away.

"That's where I saw them fighting, and he dragged Jimmie off that way," I said, indicating a line of trees.

We walked through the woods, and Mr. Kraus scoured the area like a blood hound, searching for any clues. We came to a dirt road that ran between properties and then went back out to the road.

"Looks like he parked here, expecting you to come through on your bike. But when you didn't, he got antsy and snuck through the woods over to the tree house."

He frowned, scratching his chin.

"Let's go back to the truck."

After parking the truck back in the driveway of the Kraus house, we got out and walked over by the side of the barn to sit in the shade on the bed of a hay wagon.

I asked him to tell me what he knew about Sheriff Lewis. "He's had an unusual and interesting background." "Probably normal for around here," I said with a smile.

"He was a baby, maybe eight months old, when he was adopted. His real father took off before his birth, and his birth mother already had six other children from four different men. So, she put him up for adoption, and the Lewis's here in the county became his parents. It worked out since Mrs. Lewis couldn't have any children."

"Did he ever look for his birth father?" I asked.

"No, Junior didn't want anything to do with him."

"Junior? The sheriff's name is Junior?"

"Well, technically it's Luther, but we all know him as Junior. Something you may not know is Junior's dad—his adoptive father—was a history teacher and boy's baseball coach at Fort Atkinson High School. And Junior became a stand-out pitcher for Fort Atkinson. In fact, he pitched a no-hitter to win the Wisconsin State High School Division A

Championship. Then he went on to the majors for twelve years, helping to win the World Series for the Yankees twice."

"So, how did he go from big league baseball player to become the sheriff?"

"Well, after winning his last World Series, trouble was beginning to catch up with him. He had called his birth father a dead-beat dad in the press, but it turned out Junior had fathered nine children in nine different cities when he was in the major leagues."

"So, kinda 'like father, like son.'"

Mr. Kraus nodded. "You could say that. He finally came back here to live once his baseball career ended, then went into the police academy before he decided to run for county sheriff after the long-time sheriff retired. He won by a landslide. It was like he couldn't do any wrong. It's odd, considering his kind of double life. But people here in Walworth County adore him."

"What happened to those nine kids?"

"Nothing. He said, 'All the women knew upfront what they were getting into. I have no regrets.'" Mr. Kraus paused. "Fame and fortune will change people, not always for the better."

A car pulled in the driveway. It was Rachel.

"I hope they found Jimmie," I said.

We watched her get out of the car and walk our way.

"Any good news?" I asked.

"No, not yet. But we did find the vehicle he was driving."

"Where was it?"

"Parked just off the road within walking distance of the Wendorf property."

"We found where a vehicle was parked on the dirt road close to the tree house," Mr. Kraus said.

"Yes, it appears somebody was parked there from what the investigators discovered," Rachel said.

Looking to Mr. Kraus, Rachel asked:

"I would like to have a minute and speak to Dustin alone."

"Sure, I'll be in the house if you need me," Mr. Kraus said, heading inside.

Rachel managed to hoist herself onto the back of the wagon next to me. "I want to talk to you about something you said earlier."

"Okay."

"You said Ben shot himself. Why did you say that?"

I frowned, looking down at my hands. "Jimmie told me he witnessed Mr. Wendorf shoot himself."

"Was Jimmie inside the house?"

I nodded. "He said he snuck in to take some food, and that's when he saw Mr. Wendorf napping in his recliner with the pistol by his side. Mr. Wendorf suddenly woke up, grabbed the gun, pointed it to his head, and pulled the trigger. Jimmie said he rushed over, but it was too late."

Rachel nodded. "I understand why you struggle with not knowing. The truth is, as Ben grew older, his symptoms gradually worsened. Inside the sealed envelope Jimmie took to Texas was a written confession by Ben saying he could no longer continue to live due the pain he was suffering... if he didn't die first from all his other issues."

I sighed. "Jimmie told me he believes Abby's still alive. Do you think so?"

"I don't know yet. But if she is alive, we'll find her."

"In a dream I had, my father said she is still alive."

She looked at me. "Did you ever have dreams involving Ben?"

I nodded. "Yes. Ben said in a dream that under the oak tree is the only place he felt calm, safe, and at peace. He called it magical."

"Magical?"

"He said—in the dream—that the only reason he moved back from Texas was because under the oak tree was the only place he could momentarily escape the pain."

"Interesting," Rachel said. "The attorney in Texas said that Ben's great-grandfather, Eddie, buried Edith under the oak tree. Eddie also placed an ancient cross somewhere near Edith's headstone."

"Maybe the cross has secret healing powers or something?" I said.

Rachel smiled. "Maybe." Then she looked off. "Ben did suffer his whole life from that horrific accident. My mother once told me that after she remarried Ben's dad and they moved to Texas, Ben would get violent and harm himself, saying, 'I hate living in Texas.' So, after he turned eighteen, they made special arrangements to move back here to Wisconsin. See, Ben was diagnosed and treated for different types of medical conditions and brain disorders. He even developed phobias, like nosocomephobia and peniaphobia."

"The name escapes me," I said, "but Mr. Kraus told me about some type of phobia Ben had—being scared of animals."

"Zoophobia. Yes...that too. Nosocomephobia is being afraid of hospitals and doctors. Some people call it 'white coat syndrome.' And peniaphobia is the fear of poverty, or having no money. That's why he saved every penny."

"Mr. Wendorf was sure misunderstood by people around here. Including me."

"Me too, I must admit," Rachel said.

We both sat in silence, dangling our feet off the hay wagon. I was mentally trying to put the final pieces of Mr. Wendorf's life together. He suffered from things far deeper than anyone could ever comprehend.

In a soft voice, Rachel said: "Francis took good care of my mother after my father got killed. My mother's heart was broken until she met him. She loved Texas and being with Francis on the ranch."

She paused, looking wistful as she stared into the blue sky.

"Even after my mother moved away and got remarried, she had red roses placed on my father's grave on their anniversary. After she passed, Ben took it on, like a badge of honor."

"Where is your father buried?" I asked.

"In the cemetery behind your father's church. He is buried by his own mother and father."

"You'll have to show me someday where he is buried."

Rachel nodded. "I will."

After a moment of reflection, the gears reengaged back into the present. "Well, I better get going. I find anything, I will let you know," Rachel said.

"Thank you."

"In the morning, read the newspaper. I think you will find something in there very interesting."

CHAPTER 15

Mr. Kraus and I sat in the diner, the sound of clinking silverware and conversation floating in the restaurant.

Mr. Kraus passed over the morning newspaper.

ARSON FOUND AS CAUSE OF DOUGLAS HOUSE FIRE

I absorbed every word of the article.

According to Richmond Fire Chief Dan Phillips, Al Bennett, thirty-nine years of age, of Bennett's Realty in Richmond, was formally charged with the arson.

Phillips could not divulge additional information about the details of the arson but did say video surveillance helped with the identification.

I paused.

Video surveillance? From where? What? Who?

"The incident is still under investigation, so we cannot release further details without potentially compromising the situation," Phillips said.

Mr. Kraus had already read the article, so he just sat back and watched me. The diner was about half full but still a bit noisy.

"What do you think?" he asked.

"No wonder the realty sign went missing from the front yard," I said.

"Getting rid of the evidence."

"Why would he want to burn my house down?" I asked.

Mr. Kraus shrugged. "It's only a matter of time before we find out why."

"Maybe that's why he was so nervous and acted strange at his mother's funeral."

"Yeah, he might have worried that we knew. But I wonder what else he knows?"

Jimmie

I struggled to open my eyes, but one of them was swollen shut. The other only saw darkness—no light, nothing to see.

I tasted of blood, which seemed to make my dry mouth worse.

Various parts of me hurt to varying degrees, including just breathing.

What I did know—I think—was that I was laying on a floor.

Where am I? How long have I been here?

My mind was fuzzy.

I tried to stretch out my legs, but my feet touched a wall that allowed me to only go halfway.

My wrists were handcuffed.

I reached my arms over my head, and I felt another wall.

My stomach rolled over, and I turned my head to throw up.

That hurt both my abdomen and my chest.

I worked my way up to a sitting position.

My stomach twisted again, and I vomited and vomited until there was nothing else to throw up.

Outside, I heard keys rattle and a deadbolt slide open. A sudden bright light flooded the room, and I was blinded.

I squinted open my one eye and saw I was in something like a closet.

I recognized the woman, but it took me a moment to remember...

Dustin's mother hovered over me. Up behind her came the sheriff. They both looked at me like I was a bug.

She slammed the door closed, followed by the deadbolt being re-locked. I heard her muffled voice:

"That's not Dustin! That's his dumb-ass friend Jimmie! You grabbed the wrong kid. *What the hell is wrong with you?!?!*"

She screamed that last part.

"It was dark. I saw someone come out of the tree house. I thought it was him."

"So, what are you going to do?"

A pause. "I don't know yet."

"Well, I do."

I began to hear what sounded like distant crying. It seemed to be coming up through the floor beneath me.

Then I was startled by something I perceived to be moving inside the closet. It was a kind of slithering sound.

I reached over as best I could, discovering what felt like a cable running along the wall.

I grabbed hold of it.

It felt like somebody was gently pulling it back and forth.

I heard a single knock, followed by a raspy whisper of a girl's voice. *"Hello?"*

"Hello?" I whispered back.

"Please...help me...please." She was whimpering.

"Who are you?"

"Jennifer...who are you?"

"Jimmie."

"Jimmie who?"

"Jimmie Becker."

A pause.

"Please help me...it's cold down here."

"Where are we?" I asked.

"A church, I think. Please...I'm thirsty."

Then there was the muffled sound of...a door? Then a chuckle. I could hear a deep, muddled voice.

"Did you miss me?"

I was pretty sure it was the sheriff.

"Show me how much you missed me," he said.

"No, please...stop!"

Then silence.

Dustin

Mr. Kraus ordered biscuits and sausage gravy. I had scrambled eggs, hash browns, and bacon.

We talked in between bites about why Mr. Bennett would commit arson. It was hard to understand or even come up with any type of explanation. Mr. Kraus had the idea that maybe someone paid him to do it.

When we got back to the Kraus residence, Rachel and Mrs. Kraus were seated at the table, and Emma was finishing up washing breakfast dishes at the sink. I noticed there was a newspaper on the table and a small TV on a stand in the corner.

"Why would Mr. Bennett want to burn down my house?" I asked Rachel.

"We don't know yet," she said. "But they say he is talking."

"The paper said he was identified using video surveillance. We never had anything like that."

"No. But we do."

I thought about this. "Maybe you could help me understand who 'we' are."

She offered a small smile. "'We' are a small group of people who have had our eye on this town for a while."

"So, cameras were set up to monitor our house?"

"Yes. And your tree house."

"Why?"

She frowned slightly. "Let's just say...we were concerned."

"I had no clue."

"Neither did Mr. Bennett. The night before the fire, we witnessed a dark-haired female going up inside your tree house in the middle of the night. She went up and quickly came back down. The video has some flaws and is hard to make out, but maybe you can take a look?"

Rachel turned to the TV and pressed a button on the VCR beneath it.

A dark, fuzzy image showed someone walking in the driveway where my house once was. The figure seemed to have long hair and was wearing a dress. Sandals. She stopped at the base of the tree house, then went up and disappeared. A few moments later, she came back down.

Rachel played it a couple more times.

She looked at me.

"Any idea?"

Jimmie

After a long silence, the wire began to wiggle again. I grabbed it to let her know I was on the other end. *"Jimmie...Jimmie."*

"Yes. Are you okay?"

"I will be...if you can get me out of here."

"I'm locked in a room," I said. "How often does he see you?"

"A couple times."

I felt sick again.

For a girl like Jennifer...I could only imagine how bad it might be.

"How long have you been here?"

"Four or five days, I guess. The days and nights are running together. I'm really thirsty."

"Did he...visit you before you got here?"

"Yes."

"Where?"

"The Meyer House. I'm one of the 'girls.'"

"Girls? Did you say 'girls'?"

Dustin

I took a deep breath. "At first, I thought it might be Abby Meyer, but I only saw her a couple of times. And I think that person in the video looks to be a little older and taller than Abby."

Rachel opened a folder in front of her and passed out photos of different girls. She asked if any of us could identify any of them.

Emma pointed to the third photo. "She looks like the girl in the video."

Mrs. Kraus said, "I agree."

Both Mr. Kraus and myself nodded our heads in agreement.

Mr. Kraus asked: "Do you know who she is?"

"Yes, we believe so. Her name is Jennifer Thompson, an inmate at Sugar Creek Women's Correctional Institution."

"An inmate?" Mr. Kraus asked.

"We are investigating her background," Rachel said.

"Why would she go to my tree house?" I asked.

"I was hoping you could tell me."

I shook my head. "I don't think I know anyone named Jennifer."

"She's such a beautiful child," Mrs. Kraus said, her finger tracing the photo.

"It's amazing how such a young lady could get herself into prison," Rachel said. "Let me show you the remaining photos to see if you can identify any of the others?"

We started going through them, and I stopped.

"That's Abby!" I said, pointing.

"Are you sure?"

"Absolutely! That's her!"

Jimmie

"Jimmie...Jimmie."

"Yes."

"Please get me out of here...please save me."

I managed to get up, slowly stand. It both hurt and felt good to stretch my body.

I felt around inside the walls for...anything. Something.

On the ceiling, I could feel what seemed like wood frame. On my tippy-toes, my fingertips slightly moved a piece of something.

With every bit of strength I had, I crouched down, then jumped up to push the piece away.

It moved a little but went back into its original position.

I did it a couple more times until finally, a piece of drywall came crashing down on me.

Exhausted, I collapsed back down on the floor.

I wiggled the wire.

I didn't bother to whisper. "Jennifer!...Jennifer!"

But...only silence.

Dustin

"The last known place Jennifer Thompson was seen was at the Meyer house."

Confused, I asked: "You said she was in prison, at Sugar Creek."

"She was paroled on good behavior and assigned to the Meyer House for further rehabilitation." Rachel paused. "I also think it would be best—for your protection—if you didn't visit your tree house for a while. We will be installing video surveillance equipment nearby."

She checked the clock on the wall, then gathered her things.

"There is going to be a special announcement on the five o'clock news. You may want to watch," she said before leaving.

Even before 5:00 pm, we were all sitting in the Kraus living room to watch the local news. After mentioning some stories they'd be covering—a bust of a meth operation in Walworth County, an escape of thirteen cows that invaded downtown Richmond, and a promise of "even warmer weather on the way"—the news anchor said:

> *"We begin tonight with breaking news. After a week-long search, a missing sheriff deputy has been found. Rick Baird has a live report for us."*

> *"Yes, Doug, Officer Raymond Mullin has been found by the US Federal Marshalls in an undisclosed area of Walworth County. Authorities say he has been placed into the Federal Witness Protection program but did not explain why. They did say Mullin appears to be in good health and is fully cooperating with them. We will provide additional information when more is made available..."*

CHAPTER 16

Jimmie

While I was still locked in a closet, I was trying to find a way out. Not just for me but for a mystery girl named Jennifer.

I stared up toward the opening in the ceiling where I pushed away a part of it...only to be confronted with more darkness. Not even a glimmer of light.

I sat on the floor to gather my thoughts, consider my confinement, a possible escape...and Jennifer.

Why was I kidnapped?

Apparently, the sheriff had thought I was Dustin. Which was funny since I was shorter and looked nothing like him.

What did Mrs. Douglas have to do with this? And why did she want to have the sheriff kidnap her son?

And why had she called me a dumb ass?

She wanted me dead...like throwing a bag of unwanted trash into a dumpster never to be seen or thought of again.

Was the sheriff going to gag me, tie a cinder block to my ankles, and throw me into the river? Suffocate me? Strike me with a blunt object? Or maybe he'd have a brief moment of mercy and shoot me in the back of the head so I would easily fall into the grave he dug in the woods.

Dustin's life must be...a different kind of hell. He seemed so confused, like a guy who got lost and couldn't figure out where to go.

But of all the mysteries, the one that really worried me was when Jennifer said she's one of their "girls."

What does that mean?

I shivered, feeling repulsed.

Maybe it was thinking of Sheriff Creepy, or whatever his name is, that caused my pinballing thoughts to bounce to another scenario. He kind of reminded me of the men who would drop my half-drunk mother off early in the pre-dawn morning while Dad was on one of his trucking jobs. Her hair would be a mess, blouse half unbuttoned, bra and underwear stuffed into her purse. She'd rush into the house, softly closing the door behind her, then tip-toe into the bathroom to brush her teeth and clean herself up before sneaking into my bedroom to gently rub my shoulder and say: "Good morning, sunshine...time to wake up." Then she'd kiss my forehead to get me up to get ready to catch the school bus.

What she didn't know was I had been peeking out the window, waiting for her to come home. I guess we were both well-rehearsed in playing our parts. The fresh sent of Colgate toothpaste still made me relive those nights. It's a scent that would most likely haunt me for the rest of my life.

Then I thought of Abby. It was a thought that wasn't filled with so much self-pity.

Thinking of her gave me strength and hope.

I had the strong feeling she was alive...but was she? If so, where was she? Was she in hiding, or—like Jennifer and me—trapped somewhere? Jennifer might know. She said she had been at the Meyer House, like Abby.

I had to escape the hellhole I was in. I needed to find the strength to claw my way out.

I had to get to Jennifer.

Dustin

With my mind zigzagging through a minefield, I didn't sleep.

Where would the sheriff take Jimmie? Why? Was he still alive? Was he being hurt or tortured?

I knew Jimmie was a survivor, having to grow up independently, fending for himself. But could he survive?

Was Abby still alive as Jimmie believed?

The girl...Jennifer...caught on video going up into the tree house before the fire. She may have been the one who placed the note from Abby for me to find.

It's time for dinner!

⟿⟿

Oh...my mother. What had she done? What was she doing? She may have given birth to me, but the word *Mother* didn't seem to fit her anymore. Like a snake, she had shed her parental skin.

I then imagined good ole Al Bennett's face behind bars. I was glad they arrested the pompous ass. I almost wished it was for something else, for something bigger than burning my home and tree house down.

And now they'd found Officer Mullin—the guy who had been instructed to burn my tree house down.

Why was everyone so interested in my tree house? Leaving notes, moving it, trying to burn it. Until I stopped him and his chubby partner, who knows how much further they would have gone? And I seemed to have somehow instilled a fear into them...a fear that I seemed to have magically generated—because it wasn't something I intended. It was a fear that came from somewhere deep inside myself...or it was my prayers being answered, scaring them off with their tires squealing off down the pavement?

I sighed and closed my eyes.

This had all been so...confusing. Hard. Disorienting.

Tears slid down the side of my head.

I missed my father. I missed the calmness he instilled into his conversations. I missed the quiet thoughtfulness of his actions.

In my dreams of him, he was standing in a purplish fog or haze...and he seemed to be guiding me.

I rolled over to the edge of the bed and reached under for the wooden case. I slipped it out, flipped open the lid, and pulled out the engine of the train. My fingertips slowly turned the wooden wheels around and around.

The memories of my father flooded me as more tears rolled down my cheeks.

But at least they were joyful.

Yet I began to recognize the grief I felt still trapped in my heart.

Everything had rushed by so fast since his death. It was so unfair to him. To me. The man who taught me the simple moral values of life. The man who was my rock, who I respected and proudly looked up to. A man who loved me unconditionally and made me feel safe. That man was now gone.

A painful, dark hole surrounded me, trying to make its way into my heart, into my soul.

The wheels of the train go round and round...

I began to shake with sadness, missing his gentle voice of reason.

My eyes closed, and I began hugging the wooden engine tightly, as if I were hugging him. A hammering sound came into my head...and I slipped into an image of my father's face beaming with pride. He was up on a ladder after hammering in the final nail of my tree house.

He looked back down to me as I looked up.

"Isn't it magnificent?" he asked.

I was smiling from ear to ear, but I'll never forget what I was thinking...

"Yes," is what I said.

So are you! is what I thought.

The tears rolled off my cheeks as I wept in sorrow, squeezing the train engine to my chest.

And, oh, the pain of how I missed him sank into me so deep.

Jimmie

After, using a coat hanger, I was finally able to unlock the cuffs. I jumped up several times, desperately trying to hold onto the little ledge to pull myself up into the opening while my feet swung in the air below.

But after each failed attempt, my fingers stretched...and my arms ached...with more and more pain. And more futility.

Sweat began to stream down my face.

Frustrated, I stood, leaning back against the wall, breathing hard, eyes shifting around as my brain strategized an escape.

How was I supposed to get the hell out?

I was in danger, and it seemed that it would only get worse.

Adrenaline raged, swelling to a frenzy.

Dustin

I woke up still hugging the engine of the train tightly to my chest.

At least my mind had taken a break, but it quickly began spinning again.

I rolled over to put the engine back into its case, then slid it back under the bed.

2:57 am.

I laid in bed, still engulfed in darkness.

I could hear my heart beat in my ears.

Jimmie was in big trouble...in danger...and needed help.

Jimmie

I decided if I couldn't go up...

I turned my back to the wall and began kicking backwards through the drywall, letting out a scream.

With determined force, my leg pumped my boot back and forth like a jackhammer. Cracks of dim light began to be revealed as I kicked my way through the second sheet of drywall.

Then, a hole. The freshness of cool air flooded into my little closet.

Using my hands, I ripped off the remaining pieces of drywall, clearing my way to slide out between the wall studs.

Dripping in sweat, I squeezed myself out, covered in drywall dust.

I scanned the room. It was dark, no lights, but I could see I was in an office—desk, bookcase, a couple of chairs.

I stepped toward the desk and found a light. I turned it on and saw a clock reading 3:15.

Since was dark outside, that meant middle of the night.

I ran to the door, opened it, and found a hallway with a pair of door-ways at the end. A green EXIT sign over one of the doors.

I wanted to leave, run outside, run away...but I needed to find Jennifer.

I looked down and noticed my boots had left tracks of drywall dust.

Shit.

I unlaced them and pulled them off, and as the second came off, I heard a door open, then close.

I quickly darted through the nearest doorway, which led to a kitchen.

I put the boots on the floor next to the refrigerator.

Hearing footsteps, I panicked and went to the other side of the fridge.

I saw doors. A pantry. I opened it and slipped inside.

I could peek through the crack of the doors.

The hallway light flicked on.

Then, a voice: "Oh, shit. That little bastard got out!"

The sheriff.

The kitchen door swung open, hard, slamming against the wall.

From his shadow, I could tell he had his gun drawn.

He turned on the light.

I stood frozen. I wasn't even sure if I took a breath.

The sheriff started opening the cupboards and doors under the sink.

I'm doomed. He'll check this next.

Then, suddenly, he bolted back into the hallway, and I could hear him opening all the doors out there.

I dared to open the pantry doors a little and briefly saw the back of the sheriff before he went out of view.

Then he rushed back, re-entering the kitchen.

Out of frustration, he kicked my boots across the room.

"Son of a bitch!"

He stood in the middle of the room, huffing and puffing.

"When I find...that shit...I'm going to...kill the little bastard!"

The sheriff turned, left the kitchen, and started turning on lights, looking through the other rooms in the building. He sounded farther away.

Now's my chance.

In my socks, I scurried across the kitchen, into the hallway, and quickly down the stairs to the basement.

I slipped behind a furnace to hide.

I could hear the sheriff's footsteps going back and forth at the top of the stairs.

There was some light in the basement, but not much.

I peeked around the furnace, looking for Jennifer.

I saw a door.

I heard the slamming of a door from upstairs, sounding kind of far away. Like the sheriff had left the building.

Or maybe that was what he wanted me to think.

But then I heard a car engine roar on before it took off and faded into the distance.

I came out from behind the furnace, heading straight toward the door.

It was locked. Of course.

There was a yellow sign on the door with black letters:

Electrical Room

I stepped back and kicked at the door. But it wouldn't budge.

Again. Nothing.

Again, nothing.

One more time, and nothing.

I looked around, saw some tools on a workbench, but no hammer. I did find a pipe wrench.

I hit the doorknob with it several times as hard as I could.

After fifty or sixty times, it finally gave a little. Then the knob fell off. I backed up and kicked open the door.

Jennifer was curled up on the cement floor. She was only in her underwear.

I knelt down and rolled her over. She was just skin and bones. I grabbed her wrist, my fingers feeling around. I found a pulse. "Jennifer! Jennifer! It's Jimmie." No response.

I grabbed her lifeless body and...well, it looked easier in the movies. She was all limp and wiggly, and I had to be careful not to drop her and make things worse. I managed to wrangle her up onto my shoulder.

I plodded my way over to the stairs and plunked my way up a step at a time, holding onto Jennifer for dear life.

Upstairs, I went straight for the outside door. Once in the fresh air, I saw we had been in a church. Mr. Douglas's church.

I headed across the parking lot toward the woods, and once there, I placed her onto the ground to catch my breath and get my bearings.

I need to keep going.

I hoisted Jennifer's body back on my shoulder and went deeper into the woods.

Hurrying as best I could under branches and around trees, my feet were nothing but sharp pain from stepping on twigs and rocks since I was wearing only my socks. But I kept going.

Finally, I made it to a car parked not far away. I dropped to my knees and gently placed Jennifer on the ground. I opened the car door and was thankful to see keys dangling in the ignition. Then I returned to Jennifer.

I saw her slightly move her arm. Then she tried to move her lips to say something.

I put my ear close to her mouth.

"Help...me...please...help...me..."

Her eyes opened slightly.

"I'm Jimmie—do you remember me?"

"Yes."

"I'm going to get you help."

"Where am I?"

"You're safe. The sheriff isn't going to hurt you anymore."

She shut her eyes. "Thank you..."

Dustin

As I entered the kitchen, Mr. Kraus came in from outside holding a newspaper. He'd probably fetched it from the box by the road, as usual.

It was still dark outside. The clock on the kitchen wall was pointed at 4:47.

"Good morning," Mr. Kraus said. "You're certainly up early."

"Didn't sleep well."

He nodded and opened up the paper so I could see the headline.

Officer Found Dead

"Which officer?"

He scanned the article. "Officer Sanders, Mullin's partner."

"What happened?"

He sat down and began to read.

"A hiker on a trail in Kettle Moraine Park found a pair of black boots neatly placed on the side of the path. They appeared to be the type of boots a police officer would wear—not hiking boots. The hiker said the manner the boots were left was unusual, so he scouted around and found a body off the trail. Authorities identified the body as Officer Morris

Sanders, apparently the victim of a self-inflicted gunshot wound. The coroner will determine the cause of death.

"David Zundel from the US Federal Marshalls field office is the lead investigator. 'The incident is currently being fully investigated,' is all Marshall Zundel would say."

Mr. Kraus looked up from the paper.

"I wonder why Officer Sanders would take his own life?"

Jimmie

It was difficult to get Jennifer's body up into the tree house without sending both of us to the ground. I went very slow and steady, and after several minutes, we came up through the opening in the floor, and I laid her down softly.

I took a moment to catch my breath, then lit the candle.

"Where am I?"

"Safe. We're in Dustin's tree house."

"Dustin? Tree house?"

"Yes. No one knows we're here. You won't get hurt."

"Thank you...for helping me."

"I'm looking for Abby. Do you know where she is?"

"Yes."

"Where is she?"

"At the Meyer Estate. She's hidden under the garage floor."

CHAPTER 17

Jimmie

I ran and ran...but I had to stop to catch my breath. I sat behind a tree, closing my eyes. When I opened them, I saw my socks were bloody from running through the woods and stepping on everything. Oddly, I didn't feel any pain—my feet felt numb. I guess my brain couldn't register the pain by my strong desire to find Abby.

I tried to remember what Dustin had told me about the property.

I looked out and could just make out the house.

I needed to reposition myself closer to get a better view of the area.

Dustin

The phone rang, and Mr. Kraus got up to answer it.

Mrs. Kraus had joined us at the kitchen table and was lazily stirring cream into her coffee.

"Hello?...Yes...oh hi...really? Where?...I see...okay, good, thanks for calling."

Mrs. Kraus and I both watched Mr. Kraus.

"That was Rachel. They've found the Jennifer girl."

"Oh good," Mrs. Kraus said.

"Where?" I asked.

He looked at me solemnly. "In your tree house."

I blinked in surprise.

"I would guess," Mr. Kraus said, "that the video surveillance spotted her. Rachel said the investigators found her there."

Half an hour later, Rachel walked in.

"Good morning," she said.

"So, tell us what's going on. The girl was found?" Mrs. Kraus asked.

"Yes, Jennifer Thompson was found this morning in the tree house. She is suffering from malnutrition, dehydration, and sexual abuse. She has been taken to the emergency room in Fort Atkinson, where she is currently in intensive care. Once she is in stable condition, she will be transported back to Sugar Creek's medical facility to recover."

She looked at me. "Can you help bring in the video player for me? It's in the car.

"Sure." I jumped up and fetched the bulky gadget from the backseat and brought it in.

Rachel plugged in cables and turned it on.

"This is the video surveillance tape from this morning, and there is a...well, let's say a person of interest carrying her up into the tree house. Hopefully, you can help identify them."

The video played in an eerie green glow.

We saw two people—one over the shoulder of the other—walking up to the base of the tree, and then very slowly scaling it. The quality of the images was not completely clear.

"That's Jimmie!" I said.

"It looks like he's wearing only socks," Mrs. Kraus said.

"Are you sure that's Jimmie?" Rachel asked me.

"Pretty sure."

"What time was this?" Mr. Kraus asked.

Rachel pointed to the screen. In the lower right corner, the numbers said 4:12:34.

"4:12 am," Rachel said.

Jimmie

Once my heart settled down from running, I began to think more clearly, and thankfully, my swollen eye was beginning to see a little clearer too.

Then I saw movement out the side door of the house.

The sheriff was holding what appeared to be a heap of clothes, hurrying to a car in the driveway. He tossed it in the backseat, then ran back into the house. He came out again with another armload and tossed it in as well.

Now's my chance.

I snuck up toward the driveway, picking up a thick, broken branch along the way. It was as big around as a baseball bat. I hid behind a tree nearest to the car.

The sheriff came again with another armful of stuff.

Once he walked up to put it in the backseat, I raced up behind him and smashed the branch as hard as I could against the back of his head.

He made an O*OMMFF* sound before collapsing like a sack of shit on the ground.

I stood over him for a moment, watching to make sure he was out, and he didn't move. I removed the handcuffs from a leather poach on his belt. I yanked his arms behind him and clicked on the bracelets.

I grabbed his feet and tugged, discovering he was much heavier than I'd anticipated. I managed to pull him along the ground, face-down, until

I got to a lamp post. I hoped the rough surface of the driveway would leave a scar or two. After what he did to me, to Jennifer, he deserved worse.

I found plastic zip-ties on his belt and tied them around his ankles, then to the post. Just as I yanked the second one tight, Dustin's mother came charging out the door, screaming like a banshee, straight at me.

Dustin

The video continued to play, though nothing happened for several minutes.

Then someone scooted down the tree and ran off toward the woods.

Two things I could tell: It was a male, and I was convinced it was Jimmie.

Mr. Kraus said, "I wonder where he's running off to?"

"I think I know where," I said.

Rachel looked at me. "The Meyer House?"

I nodded and got up.

"Dustin," Rachel said. "Stay here."

I shook my head.

"Sorry. I can't."

And before anyone could do or say anything, I shot out the door.

"Stop, Dustin!" is all I heard as I raced off into the early morning light.

Jimmie

Mrs. Douglas ran into me full force, knocking me over before hitting and kicking me.

I fell onto my side and put up my arms to my head to try to protect myself.

She landed a dozen slaps on me before I realized that was all she had.

I rolled onto my back and kicked my legs out, feet hitting squarely on her hips.

She went flying back like a ragdoll, arms in the air.

My adrenaline overflowed. I jumped up and launched myself at her, landing on top of her. I placed my hand over her face.

It didn't stop her. She was like a wild hyena, snarling and biting me. Her jaw clamped down on the side of my hand, and I yelped as she pushed me off and rolled on top of me.

Her fingers found my throat and began squeezing.

The pain was horrific.

My bulging eyes saw something behind her, swinging out of the sky.

The handle of a broom slammed down on top of her head with a loud, distinct cracking sound. I'm not sure if the sound came from the wood of the handle or her skull.

The unconscious body of Mrs. Douglas fell to the side.

I laid there trying to breathe and saw one of the girls from the house holding the broom from its bristles, hitting Mrs. Douglas again and again.

I rolled onto my side, wheezing as another girl—then another—came out of the house, kicking and pummeling her.

They swarmed, converging like hornets.

I managed to get to my feet, and another girl handed me some rope.

"Okay, okay," I said to the angry girls. "Stop!" I yelled just as one landed a fierce kick to the face of Mrs. Douglas.

I began tying her arms and legs up.

"Where's Abby?" I asked as I tried to make a decent knot.

"She's under the garage floor," one of the girls said.

I stood up. "Show me."

I followed her into the garage.

The girl pointed to an old metal filing cabinet along the back wall.

I pushed the cabinet aside and saw a steel plate in the floor.

I pulled it away to find a wooden ladder leading down.

I made my way down into the darkness. There was a single dim light bulb, but it was enough to see a crudely-built holding pen. Inside was

Abby, sitting in a corner, arms hugging her knees. I realized she was naked and had red swollen marks all over her body.

I pulled on the door, but the cell was locked.

Abby pointed to the wall behind me, and I saw a key on a hook. I grabbed it, unlocked, and opened the door.

I reached my hand out to help her up.

We got to the ladder and climbed it.

"There are clothes in the back of the car," I said as got out.

Several girls rushed to get them while others hugged and held Abby... and I had to think what to do next.

Dustin

As I approached the Meyer House through the woods, I saw several police vehicles surrounding the area, lights flashing and swirling. Men in uniform walked here and there, and I saw two of them escorting another uniformed man toward a car. I recognized the man in the middle.

The sheriff.

They had him.

Another car pulled up to the scene, and I recognized Rachel getting out.

I hurried over.

She pointed at me as I approached.

"You, young man, shouldn't have done that."

"I know."

She stared at me for a moment, then her expression lightened up.

"Come on," she said. "Let's let them do their job."

We got in the car and drove back to the Kraus house.

When we walked into the kitchen, Emma was sitting at the table, crying.

"What happened?" Rachel asked.

"She's gone. Gone."

"Who?" Rachel asked.

"After watching the TV news, she went into the spare bedroom...to sit in the rocking chair."

That was the room I was staying in, I thought.

"She said she wanted to be alone and sit by the window."

"What happened, Emma?" Rachel said.

"Mr. Kraus helped her into the rocking chair and pulled out the wooden train set from under the bed. He gave her the engine to hold. She thanked him and said she loved him so much. He left her alone...and when I went in to check on her...she had passed on."

My heart dropped.

Both Rachel and I walked to the spare room.

Mr. Kraus was sitting on a chair beside his wife. One hand was holding hers.

He looked up at us with swollen eyes.

"She's gone home to see Michael."

He stood up, then slowly walked past us, out the kitchen door.

"Please, oh dear Lord, comfort our friend," Rachel said as she slowly approached Mrs. Kraus.

My emotions swelled up, and I turned, walking out to the kitchen. I fell into a chair, completely overcome with tears.

Mr. Wendorf. Robert. Rusty. My dad. Officer Sanders. Maybe Abby. Now Mrs. Kraus.

It seemed my emotions had been dammed up inside me.

I felt exhausted and beat down.

The thought of Mrs. Kraus passing away was overwhelming. Even as frail as she was, she seemed so strong. I would always cherish the memories of her.

I heard the tires of vehicles crunching gravel up the driveway.

I looked out the window and saw two vehicles. One was the coroner's van. The other, a hearse.

Wow, I thought. *That was fast.*

Men exited the vehicles and were met by Mr. Kraus, Emma, and Rachel.

It wasn't long before everyone entered the house. The new visitors went into the spare room, a pair of them maneuvering a wheeled gurney through the hallway. Several minutes later, Mrs. Kraus was brought out under a white sheet.

Mr. Kraus stood silently, watching them take his wife away. Emma and Rachel stood to each side of him. Then they went out onto the porch.

When the hearse slowly pulled away and rolled out the driveway, Mr. Kraus waved good-bye.

Except it really wasn't good-bye. It was more like...*I'll see you soon.*

Mrs. Kraus had said that while at her brother's grave site.

After a couple minutes, Mr. Kraus came back in the house and looked at me.

"Emily and I were talking the other day about when her last day would come. She wanted me to ask you if you would eulogize her?"

I frowned. "I've never done that before."

"We can help you with it, if you would like. It's just telling your experiences with her. But if you feel uncomfortable, I understand."

I had to stop and think for a moment before I could answer.

"I'll be nervous, but I'd be honored. Yes. I would like to thank her for taking me in and caring for me."

Mr. Kraus nodded. "Good. Your father would be proud of you." And once again, tears welled up in my eyes.

We heard a car racing up from outside. We went onto the porch to see a sedan.

Officer Zundel got out.

"Where is Rachel?"

Rachel came out the kitchen door. "I'm here," she said.

"We got the sheriff, but Mrs. Douglas is missing."

"On the phone, you said she was at the Meyer House with the sheriff."

"Yes. That's what we thought too. But one of the girls said a young man knocked out the sheriff with a stick, then got in a fight with Mrs. Douglas. One of the girls claims she beat Mrs. Douglas off the boy with a broom. Then the boy tied her up with a rope. The boy rescued Abby Meyer, and once she was safe, the boy put Mrs. Douglas into the trunk of a car. The boy and Abby got in the car and left."

"Did they leave in the sheriff's police vehicle?" Rachel asked Zundel.

"No, it was the sheriff's private car."

Rachel turned and looked at me. "Any idea where they might go?"

I had nothing. I shrugged. The only thing I could think of was..."Texas?"

CHAPTER 18

We all stood watching as Officer Zundel got in his vehicle and raced away.

Rachel said: "He'll track them down. He's like a bloodhound."

"Jimmie was right all along," I said. "Abby is alive."

"Yes, he was. Do you remember me telling you when the time was right, I'd tell you what I know?"

"I do."

"Well...the time is right."

"We should leave you two to talk," Mr. Kraus said. Then he turned to Emma. "Will you go with me to the funeral home to help me make the arrangements?"

"Yes, of course," Emma said.

They both got into Mr. Kraus's pickup truck and rolled off toward Richmond. Both Rachel and I went into the kitchen and took seats at the kitchen table. Rachel gave a deep sigh. "It's going to take some time for me to get adjusted to not having Emily here. I will miss my dear friend."

"I know. She was so sweet. Mr. Kraus asked me to say a few words at her funeral."

"Emily lived a very meaningful life. You will find the right words. I will share with you some of my stories about her." She paused, looking me squarely in the eye. "She told me...all she wanted for you is...for you to find and accept the truth."

I frowned. "The truth seems so...so hard to determine. One person's truth is not another's. And even then, it can be so deeply hidden."

"It often is."

She looked at her watch.

"It's almost time."

She looked at me in an odd way and smiled.

"We should go for a little drive," she said. "There's something I want to show you."

"Oh. Okay."

"Would you mind driving?"

We pulled out onto the main road, heading in the direction of town.

"After law school," she said, "when I first worked as a county prosecutor, I spent years in the law libraries reading over hundreds of cases. That's when I discovered the truth is always there, just hidden behind thick walls of lies. And it was my job to find the smallest weakness or crack in the wall. I had to build my cases around lies in order to expose the buried secret."

I nodded. "I now feel my mother has hidden herself behind a thick wall of lies."

"Sounds like your instincts are right. It may be your mother fell prey and became a tool used in an elaborate and well-constructed wall of lies that she's now trapped behind."

I tilted my head, trying to understand. "What do you mean?"

"She...she became the center of attention, and she has savored every second of it. The game, the power, the money, the sex, the control. It was all for her enjoyment...until now. I've been doing some research, and it looks like it was a little over a year ago when your mother was lured in by the wink of an eye—the sheriff's eye. I've been onto him for a while, and he has no boundaries when it comes to women. It didn't matter if they were married or not. Pretty or not.

He wanted what he wanted. And it didn't begin with him. It started with an unethical judge."

"Really? A judge?"

"Yes. Judge Dru is the man who orchestrated and maneuvered all of this."

"I had no idea my mother knew the sheriff until recently. Much less any judge."

"She only knew the judge through the sheriff. The judge shielded himself and sat in the shadows in his neatly pressed black robe."

"Sounds like you never liked him."

I glanced at her, and she had a small smile.

"Go to the courthouse," she said.

A few minutes later, I pulled into the mostly empty courthouse parking lot. Since it was a Sunday, there was only a plain, black sedan near the entrance.

"After I retired from being a federal judge," she said after I parked, "I was offered and accepted a position on the board of the Wisconsin Judicial Commission. It's a division that investigates any judicial misconduct, someone who might abuse their authority. Violating laws they took an oath to faithfully uphold. I found out Judge Dru spun an invisible web of lies to enrich himself financially and feed his darkest erotic fantasies."

I let this sink in a little.

"Did Judge Dru have anything to do with my house being burned down?"

"No. That was strictly between your mother and Mr. Bennett."

"I don't understand why they did it."

"Well...everything bad usually boils down to sex or money. Mr. Bennett didn't want to confess at first, so the investigators...well, they took him to a special place...let's say a private place where they asked him some very difficult questions under some very uncomfortable circumstances."

I smiled. "By any chance, did they take him to the place under the old tool shed on Mr. Wendorf's property?"

Rachel smirked. "I don't know, I wasn't there. But some people have a very hard time telling the truth, and Al Bennett had that problem until he was shown the surveillance video. Then he spilled the beans. Apparently, your mother was upset with the sheriff's failed attempt to have it burned down, so she offered Mr. Bennett $10,000."

"She must have found it."

"Found what?

"The money!"

"What money?"

"Mr. Wendorf's money. Jimmie found it under the tool shed."

She paused. Obviously, she didn't know I knew about the money.

"No, she didn't find that—the investigators did. They discovered a crumpled map in a pair of jeans inside your house—probably yours. That was the day before the fire."

"They searched my house?"

"For good reason, obviously. But they had a search warrant, so it was by the book."

"That's a relief. I thought maybe my mother found the map or some of the money in my jeans."

"No, fortunately not."

"I saw the investigators take two people into the tool shed—Mr. Bennett and...who?"

"Officer Mullin was the other. He actually broke faster than Al Bennett did. He didn't particularly like being so...uncomfortable. He gave us some valuable evidence along with written testimony before being placed into the Witness Protection Program."

"What evidence did he turn over?"

"Abby's underwear!"

"What!?!?"

"See, they were going to use her underwear as one of the central pieces of evidence to convince the jury your father was guilty of raping, then killing her."

I sat, digesting the thought. My mother was going to use this "evidence" to frame my father.

"What about the blood at the crime scene by the river?"

"We also discovered in a sworn statement from Officer Mullin that your mother, against Abby's will, took a couple vials of her blood while she was held captive. Then she gave them to the sheriff to pour out at the crime scene. This was to be used as 'the nail in the coffin' DNA evidence to prove Abby's death."

"My mother staged the crime scene?"

"No. Officer Mullin was confused; Sheriff Lewis did."

I paused. "Okay, so at the funeral of Mr. Bennett's mother, as he was walking away, he turned to Mr. Kraus and said something very odd. 'I didn't know anything about any girls.'"

"Yes, that's a strange thing. But that's where the judge comes into play." Rachel noticed the blank look on my face as I sat...lost.

"What does the judge have to do with the girls?"

"That is where the whole investigation started. The judicial board received an anonymous claim from a whistleblower who only identified themselves as 'J.T.' That led us straight to Judge Dru. We now know J.T. is Jennifer Thompson."

"The girl they found in the tree house?"

"Yes. And she told us that she was the person who submitted the anonymous claim to the board."

"What was the claim?"

"In her statement, she detailed a brilliant and well laid-out scheme."

Rachel checked her watch, then looked out the passenger window. A few moments later, three dark-blue sedans pulled into the parking lot and stopped near the courthouse entrance. A pair of men got out of each, six in all, as well as a woman holding a briefcase. All marched up the steps and into the courthouse.

"What's that?" I asked. "What's going on?"

Rachel's facial expression and posture became rigid...focused. But she didn't say anything. We just sat and waited.

Five minutes later, the group that went in came out, but with one extra person included.

An older, white-haired man.

"What I'm about to explain to you has taken our investigators over three months to carefully unravel," Rachel said as we watched two of the men place the white-haired man in the back of a car. "The people involved in this story are both elected and appointed state and county officials—with the judge being the centerpiece to our investigation. This case will be the most deceptive and unethical abuse of power by officials ever brought forth in the state of Wisconsin. The case involves a crime circle of sex and money laundering."

"And my mother was involved in all of it?"

"Yes. She was directly involved for well over a year now."

"I had no idea."

The cars began to back out and leave the parking lot.

"Those people who just came are FBI; Justice Department; a Wisconsin State Police officer; David Zundel, the US Marshall; and the woman is a federal prosecutor."

"And the guy with the white hair? The one who looked like he was being arrested?"

"That," she said, "was Judge Dru. And yes, he was just arrested."

I paused, thinking. "So, you knew this would happen, and you wanted me to see." She nodded.

"They are on their way to arrest the head of the Department of Parole and Release Unit at Sugar Creek Women's Correctional Facility, Warden Theodore McDorman. The judge and the warden have a relationship that goes way back to their high school days. They both went through very messy divorces recently. And they were reacquainted at the governor's mansion during a birthday party two years ago.

"We believe Judge Dru and the warden met at Sugar Creek, and that's when they collaborated. We think both men abused their authority by indulging in sexual activities with select inmates at Sugar Creek. The term 'girls' was their disguised code name to describe the female inmates they abused."

She paused.

"Are you hungry?"

"Not really."

"Me either. But let's go to the diner, where it might be a better place to talk." I started the car, and we drove the few blocks to Mary Lou's.

We went inside, finding the Sunday morning crowd quite talkative. However, they seemed to quiet down as we headed to a booth. I felt like everyone was staring.

"Don't worry," Rachel said, patting the back of my hand after we took our seats. "They are all feeling bad for you."

The waitress came with a pair of water glasses and set them down. "How are you doing?" She didn't say it in the normal friendly way, but more of a concerned, worried way, as if I had just gotten out of the hospital.

I only nodded, and Rachel said "We're okay, Linda. Just here to chat."

Linda nodded. "I'll bring a couple of menus anyway. You just take your time." The volume of conversation in the diner returned as people got back to their stories. Rachel took a sip of the water. Then:

"I have a very difficult time with what I know. This is very personal to me. The predatory behavior of the judge, warden, and sheriff was evil. And it was morally disturbed men like them...they are a reason I went to law school and what led me to become a prosecutor."

Linda returned, sliding the menus onto the tabletop before hurrying away.

When she was out of earshot, Rachel continued.

"I truly understand how awful this is for you. But I promised I would tell you the truth...and believe me, sometimes the truth is worse."

I nodded. "Go on."

She watched me carefully, then took a deep breath.

"The judge wanted to be more discreet and enlisted Warden McDorman to bribe a couple of members of the parole board, allowing certain inmates to be placed into an early rehabilitation release program. Several years ago, your father put together a program with the Department of Parole at Sugar Creek to help assist young women. It was a great program, and it was named 'Faith and Freedom.' Specially selected inmates would be released into the program and stay at the Meyer House under strict rules and supervision. The mentoring conducted turned out to be extremely successful under the watchful eye of your father.

"But the demands of the church were taking your father's attention. So, he enlisted the sheriff to help oversee the program at the Meyer House."

I sat, listening intently.

"At some point shortly thereafter," Rachel continued, "your mother fell in with the sheriff."

"That's a nice way to put it."

She nodded. "Once enlisted, she was considered the final piece of their network. She was placed on a pedestal, and the men provided protection over her. The inmates at Sugar Creek would do whatever it took to get your mother's attention since she was allowed to pre-screen the girls at Sugar Creek before their release into the program and Meyer House. The selected girls would have to quietly go through a maze of men to preform sexual...duties in order to get on the list.

"Once at the Meyer House, the judge pulled strings behind the scenes. Knowing men of wealth and power, the judge would secretly negotiate lucrative cash payments for the 'girls.' Some as high as a quarter of a million dollars. The girls would be transported using a sheriff's vehicle driven by Officer Saunders. We have statements from some girls. Officer Saunders would stop along the way to force the girls to...indulge him. We believe that once he discovered we had a warrant for his arrest, Saunders ran and took his own life."

Linda approached. "Sorry to bother you, but Miss Connor? There's a phone call for you. You can take it in the back if you want."

Rachel looked confused. "Okay, thanks." She scooted to the end of the booth. "I wonder how they knew I was here."

A few minutes later, she returned.

"That was Marshall Zundel. He told me they found Jimmie and Abby."

"Where?" I asked.

"It appears Jimmie took Abby to the emergency room in Fort Atkinson."

"Is she going to be okay?"

"Zundel's on his way there, but he didn't know all the details. The hospital would only say she is in critical condition."

"What about my mother? Where is she?"

"We don't know yet. He said she is still missing." Rachel picked up her purse. "We have to go."

CHAPTER 19

I drove Rachel back to the Kraus farm, where her car was.

"I must leave you here," she said.

"Can I come along? I would like to see Jimmy and Abby."

"I know, but not yet."

We got out, and she headed for her vehicle. "Thank you," I said. "Thank you for telling me."

She only nodded and looked sad. She looked me in the eyes.

"Don't come. Please."

Then she got in her car and backed out of the driveway.

I stood there for several minutes, trying to figure out what I was supposed to do. I was so tired, and yet...so alert.

I needed...I needed...peace.

I was restless. I was desperate to escape the tension.

I knew what I needed. I could get on my bike or use my car...but I knew what I needed.

I started running. Running faster and faster. Soon, I slowed and stood on the Wendorf property. Completely out of breath, I leaned against the rear tire of the old tractor under the tree house. I took the time to gather myself. I could feel the tension release, and I began to think clearer.

A thought entered my mind.

I slowly peeked around the rear tire under the tractor, and I saw it: the marker of Mr. Wendorf's grandmother.

I knelt down and crawled under the tractor. I could make out a small concrete ground marker. I crawled in closer to pull away the weeds and grass that had grown over it.

Edith Wendorf

I carefully felt around the base of the stone but found nothing. I tilted the stone back, and under it was an iron cross.

I picked it up and wiped away the dirt. It was obviously old and heavy.

I couldn't help but wonder about its journey here. I was holding an ancient piece of religious Templar history.

It had a simple design. The symbolism was powerful.

I replaced the cross and tilted the stone back over it.

A calmness fell over me as I crawled out from under the tractor. I stood, noticing a deer casually nibbling on green leaves along the fence line about fifty yards away. It wiggled its ears and wagged its tail back and forth.

Mrs. Kraus thought the deer indicated the calming presence of her brother Michael. But this felt different. Not Michael. Maybe it was... Mrs. Kraus?

Oddly, the deer's head rose up and down, as if saying yes.

I could picture Mrs. Kraus shuffling into the bedroom I had been staying in, sitting in the rocking chair, smiling from behind her wire rim glasses.

I smiled at the deer.

"Hello, Mrs. Kraus."

The deer stared at me for a moment, then turned and walked into the woods.

I walked over and climbed up into the tree house, leaning against the wall, stretching out my legs. A peace came over me, and I closed my eyes.

A purplish hue vision filled my mind, and I sat frozen as the haze seemed to thicken. A tiny but bright light emerged from the fog and transformed into an outline of someone.

As the image became clearer, I realized it was my father walking into view.

Was this a dream or really happening? I kept my eye closed.

The fog slowly cleared, and I observed my father standing in a well-groomed garden.

"The beans are growing nicely this year," he said. "Mrs. Kraus would be delighted. She said to say hello."

"Is she okay?" I asked.

"Yes. She has been reunited with Michael."

"I didn't get a chance to say goodbye."

Father nodded. "She understands."

"How are you?" I asked.

"Doing all right."

"I miss you."

"I miss you too."

"Jimmie found Abby."

"Yes. I know."

"Is she going to be okay?"

"Yes. In time."

"Is the other girl, Jennifer, going to be okay?"

"Yes, after she recovers. She wants to make her wrongs right."

"I found an iron cross under the headstone of Mr. Wendorf's grandmother."

"You found the truth."

"Is it really from the Templars?"

"As I said, you found the truth."

"I wish Mom was more truthful. I have a lot of questions for her."

"Why don't you ask her?"

"She still missing."

"No, she's not."

"Where is she?"

"I will tell you under one condition."

"What is it?"

"You don't hurt her."

"What? After what she did to you? And to our family!"

"Dustin, you must understand—your mother has committed herself to the other side and can't return."

"What does that mean? The other side of what? Can't return from where?"

"Barbra...she destroyed her moral compass. She has entered into the hands of darkness and will be forever in the bondage of evil. It's where she wants to be."

"Where is she?"

"Before I tell you, you must stand strong and promise not to hurt her."

"Where is she?"

"You promise?"

I was so frustrated. I couldn't imagine hurting my mother...yet...I didn't know what might happen when I found her. Before I could say anything, Dad added something:

"One more thing...ask your mother...why did she beat Abby with a stick?"

"Where is she?"

"You promise?"

"Yes! Okay? Yes, I promise. Where is she?"

Dad took a couple of steps forward. Then he pointed.

I turned to look to where his finger was directed.

It was Mr. Wendorf's old tool shed.

Then Dad said: "Tell her I said hello...and I have forgiven her." When I turned back to answer, he had disappeared. He was gone. When I opened my eyes, I drew in a deep breath before releasing it.

I walked with purposeful caution toward the old shed, not knowing what expect.

I knew the vision of my dad was just a vision, a dream, and not necessarily real.

I stepped down the concrete stairs of the shed, smelling the dusty mustiness. I turned the door handle and pulled on it. It creaked just like in the movies, and inside, it was dark. I felt along the wall and found the switch. The dim bulb came on, and a chill came over me. Like a dozen black snakes were slithering all over my skin.

My mother was tied to a chair. There was what looked like duct tape over her mouth. She saw me and moved her shoulders around, trying to break free. Her swollen eyes focused on me. She appeared thinner, gaunt, and her hair that was normally pulled back was hanging down in her face. She paused, mumbling something through her taped mouth.

Frankly, I was glad I couldn't make out her gibberish.

I pulled the other chair across the floor and placed it in front of her. Apparently, I placed the chair uncomfortably close to her because she jolted her head to the side and pressed herself further back into the chair.

I decided to inch in even closer.

"Hi, Mom...Dad wanted me to tell you he says...hello. And to let you know he forgives you."

She whipped her head to the other side, eyes avoiding me.

"Dad told me you were down here."

She squirmed and said some garbled nonsense.

"You missed it, Mom! The Krauses gave me a really cool car for my birthday." I didn't smile. I could feel my palms getting hot and sweaty.

"You must have been doing something really important to miss my birthday...right?" Overcome with bitterness, I stood, shoving the chair aside. It fell, and the sound was louder than I expected.

She jerked and twisted in her chair.

I stepped behind her. I leaned down and whispered in her ear.

"The authorities have your buddy in custody."

If she had a reaction, I couldn't see it.

I saw a piece of wood laying on the floor. I stepped over and picked it up. I turned, holding it up.

My mother's eyes grew wide just before I slammed it down onto the table. The jarring sound cracked through the air like a thunderbolt.

She jolted hard, as if I had hit her...though I wasn't even close.

"Now that I have your attention...since you like playing games...we're going to play a little something. It's called Truth or Consequences. Here are the rules: I'm going to ask you a question, and you're going to tell me the truth. And if you don't tell the truth...the consequence would be this hitting you in the face."

I waited, watching her. I saw tears rise in her eyes. It didn't faze me.

"A word of warning, Mother...you might be very surprised as to what I know!" Her eyes looked from my face to the piece of wood that I was holding.

"Do you understand the rules? Nod your head if you understand. Shake your head if you don't."

She hesitated, then nodded her head.

"Good!"

I stepped back behind her, reaching around her face to rip off the tape covering her mouth.

She didn't say anything. She just let out a big breath of air.

I walked in front of her.

"First question. Who tied you up?"

She sat quietly.

I leaned in close. "I should add that not answering could lead to a consequence." She blinked at me, a single tear running down her cheek. "So...who tied you up down here?"

She looked down toward the floor. Then through tight lips, she said: "That little bastard...Jimmie."

"Interesting," I said. "That is good to know Jimmie found you. Ironic, actually. So, next question—where was Abby?"

Again, she sat quietly.

I leaned in again. "Where was Abby?"

She started crying. "I don't know where she is."

I slammed down the piece of wood on the table.

BANG!

"I don't know!" she screamed.

"Okay. Let me speak a little slower...I didn't ask, 'Where is Abby?' I asked...'Where *WAS* Abby?'"

She looked away, then mumbled: "She was hidden in the garage under the floor."

"What garage?"

"At the Meyer House."

"So, you hid her away under the garage floor...and blamed everything on Dad?"

"Yes."

"Why did you hit Abby with a stick?"

She tried to turn her head.

I lifted the piece of wood and tilted my head. Then I smacked the piece of wood down even harder on the table.

She wiggled around in her chair. "Because she messed everything up! Okay?"

"No!" I yelled. "Not okay!"

I paused, getting my temper in check.

"I understand the sheriff took a liking to you...did you know that?"

She softly said, "Yes."

I swear, I wanted nothing more than to beat her with the piece of wood. But I would honor my father's request. And my promise.

"That's right, I know all about the 'girls'!"

She looked shameful.

"Dad was right," I said. "You're not worth hurting." I tossed the piece of wood into the corner.

"I hope you rot in hell!" I said as I headed for the door.

I placed my hand on the doorknob and paused.

"Goodbye, Mother. This is the last time you will ever see me." I opened the door and slammed it shut behind me.

I went up a few steps, then sat on the stairs...and just cried.

After a while, I gathered myself and turned to walk up the last few stairs.

At the top, Rachel was standing there with Officer Zundel.

"Is there anything else you want to say to your mother before we take her away?" Officer Zundel asked.

"Now's your chance, Dustin," Rachel said.

"No. I said what I had to say."

EPILOGUE

Ten years later...1987

S am came running up, holding a pool noodle.

"Dad, can I go swimming?"

"Yep, that's why we're here. Go put on your trunks."

"Yay!" he said, jumping up and down, the pink noodle bouncing wildly.

Jenn pointed at the small pile of clothes on the cooler. "They're over there," she said. He hopped over with the exuberance only a six-year-old can have, dropped the noodle, and pulled off his T-shirt.

"Sam," I said. "Let's be modest. Go over behind those bushes to change your shorts."

"Righty-oh," he said, and his mother stifled a giggle.

"Sounds just like you," she said.

His sister, Emily, sat in the dirt nearby, running her fingers through some of it. The four-year-old glowed in the sunshine, mostly due to the layers of sunscreen her mom had slathered on. She was so fair-skinned, she was almost translucent. Her fine, thin blonde hair was an anomaly since Jennifer and I had brown hair.

Although I'd rarely come to this watering hole while growing up, that was mainly due to not having many friends who wanted to head out to this somewhat remote location. The couple of times I did go with a handful of other sixth-grade boys, one kid scraped his shin so bad on a rock that the skin flapped down, making my stomach roll. Another time, a boy nearly drowned because he didn't know how to swim. Needless to say, it didn't bring fond memories, but Jimmie had suggested it, and I didn't want to sound like a wussy.

As if on cue, a minivan came off the dirt road onto the clearing.

I stood and waved, even though I couldn't make out the people inside. A moment later, Jimmie and Abby exited in their summer clothes and sunglasses.

Since we were in high school, Jimmie had added a couple of inches to his height and had filled out physically. And Abby...

"Wow," Jennifer said. "Look at you! When are you due?"

"Next month," Abby said, sounding like she wished it was sooner. Her belly looked ready to burst.

We all hugged, smiling, commencing our annual get-together.

"Uncle Jimmie! Uncle Jimmie!" Sam said, running out from behind the bushes, arms up to receive a hug.

"Hey, Sammy!" Jimmie said, picking him up at arm's length. "Where are your pants?"

"Over there," my son said, pointing at the bushes.

"Well, you should go get them."

Sam was set down, and he ran off butt-naked to get his trunks.

Jimmie headed back to the minivan to unbuckle their two kids. Their oldest, six-year-old Rachel, was like a mini-Abby—dark hair and dimples. Their boy, Ben, four, was named after Mr. Wendorf and, fortunately, looked more like his dad than his namesake.

Both kids looked sleepy, as if they had slept during the car trip, but Rachel saw Emily and immediately came awake.

"Emmie!" she squealed, running toward my daughter, who didn't look up, still too enraptured with the dirt.

Ben stood where he was, looking lost. He was already in his swimming trunks and wore a T-shirt that read *It Wasn't Me!*

Sam came wandering out from behind the bushes, now in trunks, saw Ben, and went running over.

"Hey, wanna go swimming?"

Ben looked confused and as if he was going to cry. It had been a year since he'd last seen Sam, and he didn't recognize him.

Sam then looked confused.

Jimmie came to the rescue, scooping Ben up and whispering in his ear. Ben didn't look convinced, but he didn't appear fearful anymore.

Jennifer and Abby were having a private moment, or so I thought. I approached carefully in case I wasn't welcome.

"What do you think?" Jenn asked me.

She often did that, asking me questions as if I knew what she was talking about. "I'm all for it," I said. "Unless I'm not."

"Abby brought up a good point about the kids going to the funeral. It's more for us than for them. They might...you know."

"But Sam looks so good in his little suit," I said, trying to lighten the mood while thinking things through. "So, we need a brace babysitter."

"The problem is, it's short notice," Abby said. "And everyone will want to be there."

"It will be like your father's service," Jimmie said, still holding little Ben. "The whole town might turn out."

"Judge Rachel was special to everyone. Even her enemies admired her," Abby said.

"I can't argue with that," I said. "I'm still trying to absorb that she's gone. First Mr. Kraus last year, now her."

I felt a tug on my shirt.

"Dad..."

"Yeah, yeah, yeah. Swimming," I said.

Once Jimmie and I got the kids tired out and hungry, we sat on a giant blanket and ate sandwiches and chips.

"I hate to bring up a sore subject," Jimmie said, "but have you seen your mother?"

I shook my head. "No. You?"

"Naw. I don't know where she is. I don't think she knows where she is."

We all fell silent, all of us having gone through some form of parental trauma. Abby's parents dying in car tragedy, Jennifer's mother passing from cancer, her father in a hospice with Alzheimer's, Jimmie's father dying from unknown causes in a hotel room in Nevada, his mother disappearing into a constant alcoholic haze, my father dying in jail, my mother in prison. There were no greeting cards for this stuff.

But at least we all were trying to be the best parents we could be.

Personally, I knew it took Jennifer a long time to trust me, much less want to date me, after the ordeal she had gone through at the hands of my mother and the sheriff—not to mention the judge and the warden. When we had Sam, then Emily, she was overly protective of them and wanted to do everything herself, as if she wasn't sure about me yet. After years of therapy and talking, she finally began to relax. She still had nightmares, but they're less frequent. The truly horrible nights were the rare occasion when my nightmares happened at the same time as hers.

"How's business, Dustin?" Jimmie asked, probably sensing my thoughts were not in a good place.

"Good," I said. "I keep having to remind myself that the point is to help people, not make money, but it's the making money that helps people."

Jimmie nodded. "You changed the name, though, right? The Faith and Freedom Rehabilitation Program?"

"Just 'Faith and Freedom' now. The whole process of turning inmates into productive citizens with a future hinges on faith and freedom."

"I read that article in *The New York Times*," Abby said. "There have been more than 10,000 prisoners who have gone through the program?"

"About 12,000 now, but...yeah."

"Do all of them, you know, stay clean?"

"No, but more than not."

"You can lead a horse to water," Jimmie said.

"What a tribute to your father," Abby said.

"And it's mainly because of Emma, the Kraus's housekeeper," Jennifer said.

I nodded. "When she told me how my father saved her from a life in prison, I was floored. I mean, here's this sweet, sweet woman who would never hurt a fly, and she was telling me how she was sentenced to prison for selling narcotics." I shook my head. "And my dad gave her a glimmer of hope, and she took it."

"Don't forget Soupbone!" Jimmie said.

"Soupbone!" Abby said. "I will never forget meeting him at the funeral. The way he told that remarkable story about Pastor Douglas under heavy fire saving that little girl...it has been etched in my mind ever since."

I chuckled. "Soupbone's real name was Kevin...Kevin Davis, I think. He was a helicopter pilot Dad met while serving as a chaplain in the Vietnam War. Dad rarely ever talked about his service during the war and never mentioned anyone named Soupbone. And it turned out there was a good reason for that. When Dad came home, he was deeply troubled and emotionally scarred by an event that took place—an incident that only Soupbone knows the details to."

"Didn't he give your dad a nickname? Like...well, some bird?"

"Yes, Sparrow."

"I remember him," Jimmie said. "He limped to the podium wearing a denim-collared shirt with a black leather vest and blue jeans. He had this weathered face, like he was twenty years older than he really was. His thick gray hair hung down to his belt but was braided and pulled back."

My memories sent me back to my father's memorial service, Soupbone's hand gripping the side of the lectern to steady himself.

"I met Pastor Douglas in the chow hall one day, and we became fast friends. I often saw him praying over the severely injured or the dead as men would go back and forth to bring the soldiers back to base camp. One day, we were short-handed, and we needed someone to help load the men into the helicopters. Pastor Douglas volunteered. He jumped on the copter, and as we approached the zone and the copter came down, we took on heavy fire. I returned fire,

and it was a bloody, sad scene. Pastor Douglas jumped out once we were close enough to the ground and started running back and forth, loading the men. I was amazed as he seemed to float in between the rounds, never being hit. Both the pilot and myself took rounds. I was hit in the hip and leg."

He paused, letting it sink in.

"But the most amazing thing is when the pilot motioned with his hand to go, Pastor Douglas jumped out again to grab a little four-year-old Vietnamese girl. Back in the copter, he never stopped holding her as she slowly stopped crying from his comfort. Once back at camp, the Pastor came over to check on us as the medics attended our wounds, and the pilot said, 'Nice work, Sparrow.' That name stuck with him through his service to our country."

Soupbone limped over to a pedestal covered by a cloth. He revealed that under it was a bronze bust.

The inscription read: *Pastor "Sparrow" Douglas.*

That was when the stained-glass window begun sparkling in a brilliant purple, rays cascading throughout the church.

"Didn't he have a brother?" Jimmie asked, breaking my thoughts.

"Yes. Years later, Dad met up with Soupbone out in Oregon to go salmon fishing on the Rogue River. I don't know what was said between them, but I was told Dad came back a changed man. I was only four or five, so I don't remember. However, Dad shared it with Mr. Kraus, who passed it on to me after the funeral. Basically, it was an idea of how he could reduce the burden of incarceration cost on taxpayers. This was after the Sugar Creek Women's Correctional Institution was built here in the county."

Jimmie nodded. "That's right. That's where the brother comes in."

"I think his name was Neil," I said. "He started a facility out at the Eastern Oregon Correctional by the base of the Blue Mountains near Pendleton. Neil put together a denim garment factory for the inmates under the name 'Prison Blues.' It had the tagline 'Made on the inside to be worn on the outside.'"

Abby smiled. "I've heard of 'Prison Blues.'"

I nodded. "Today they sell to the public—denim work jeans and yard coats. It helps to help offset the tax burden housing prisoners causes the county and state. And, Mr. Kraus said Dad was passionate about the idea. He got involved and created the first step in his quest to do the same thing here. And that became the Faith and Freedom Rehabilitation Program at Sugar Creek."

"And don't forget what your dad did for Emma," Jennifer said.

"I know," I said. "She was beyond grateful."

"What did he do?" Abby asked.

"According to her, he was the only person during a very difficult time of her life, the only one willing to help her. She had been sentenced to ten years for selling narcotics and sent to Sugar Creek."

"Emma? Sweet old Emma?" Jimmie said.

"Yep. My father reached out and offered to help reshape her life—under one condition. That she must take the first step to help herself."

"And what step was that?" Abby asked.

"She decided that first step was to get an education. And she got her GED in prison. And true to his word, Dad made sure Emma was the first in the Faith to Freedom rehabilitation program. I remember her telling me how she grew up in the poverty-stricken projects of Milwaukee, and being a young girl, all she saw and heard growing up was gunshots and police sirens through the night. Her father was shot and killed shortly after she was born. Then her mother, trying to support her children, would scam the state's welfare systems."

"How'd she do that?" Jimmie asked.

"By triple-dipping the system...and she was proud of it. Plus, she could make more money selling drugs while receiving her welfare checks. All told, it was more than she could make if she worked a legitimate job."

"That must have been so hard on Emma," Abby said.

I nodded. "She said her earliest memories of childhood were never sleeping in her own bedroom in her own bed. She slept in an old smelly sleeping bag on the floor as they moved from place to place. Emma's mother would pack her and her two brothers into her old beat-up car, then drive from Milwaukee to Chicago then Detroit, then back to Chicago before returning to Milwaukee. The mother would make the kids dress up in Chicago Bears clothing so when she picked up her Illinois welfare check, it looked like they lived there. Then Detroit, where they wore Lions or Tigers shirts and picked up the Michigan welfare check. Once back in Milwaukee, they would be in either Bucks or Brewers outfits. Round and round it went."

"And it got worse," Jennifer said.

"Oh, no," Abby said.

"Oh, yes. Emma went on to realize her mother was also transporting drugs from state to state. She called it 'cash for gas money.'"

"I guess that's where Emma got into dealing drugs," Jimmie said.

I nodded. "And then, prison."

"What about the brothers?" Abby asked.

"One is in for life at Joliet State Penitentiary for shooting another guy in a bad drug deal in Chicago. And the younger brother OD'd at seventeen on heroin."

"Wow. Sometimes you just don't know the whole story," Jimmie said.

"My father promised not to tell anyone. I guess the Kraus's knew, but they kept the secret. She was released into the Faith and Freedom program a couple years before the Meyer House was established into a rehabilitation facility for female inmates."

"And what about Emma's mother?" Abby asked. "What happened to her?"

"She died from AIDS before Emma was sentenced to Sugar Creek."

"Man, what a hard life," Jimmie said.

"But it turned out better," Jennifer said. "What was that thing your dad said to her? About friends?"

"Yeah, something like, 'Don't look at me as somebody who will hurt you, or even a man. Look at me as your friend.'"

"She gave a beautiful little memorial at his service," Abby said. "But she only talked about him serving other people without mentioning one of them was her."

"It was her way to thank him publicly. He didn't want the attention or the credit. After all, *he* didn't change them—they did it."

"Tell them about the window," Jennifer said.

I smiled. "Yeah. Just before Emma received her GED, she drew this simple picture of a window. She gave it to him as he would go to the prison once a week for two years to help tutor Emma. She drew the window like some kind of metaphor for the special life he had shown her. Dad took that drawing and used it for the basis of the stained-glass windows—two in fact: one for Emma and the other for my tree house. Emma said he told her it would be a window to help remind her of her past and guide her into the future."

"Oh, how sweet," Abby said, eyes tearing up.

We sat in silence for a while before Jennifer stood up.

"It's getting dark," she said. "We should get some dinner—I was thinking about the diner."

"That sounds perfect," Jimmie said.

We began collecting our stuff and children, packing them up before heading into town.

Over hamburgers, hot dogs, and patty melts, we spent more time catching up. Abby and Jimmie split their time between here in Wisconsin and also in Texas—so Jimmie could manage the Wendorf properties, including the steer ranch, and seven oil wells. Abby oversaw the Meyer House Center's staff and programs. Plus, with being parents, they were more than busy.

They knew more about what was going on in town than I did, but so many people had passed, I wasn't sure there were people here who I would know...or who would know me.

Mr. Kraus passed last year, Rachel this year. Emma moved to Madison after the Kraus farm was sold—and I needed to make time to go visit her. I'd heard her health had been frail, which was hard to comprehend knowing how hard she worked.

We left the diner, Jimmie and Abby taking their kids to the hotel while I asked Jennifer if we could make a brief detour before heading to ours.

I pulled the mini-van into the driveway, the lights sweeping across new vegetation that was growing in the place where the Wendorf house was.

"Is this a park?" Sam asked from the backseat.

"No, but it's someplace special."

We got out, and I found the flashlights in the back I had packed away for this. I handed one to Jenn.

I carried Emily in one arm while scanning the ground with the light.

"Wow!" Sam said as the beam from Jenn's light found the tree. "What's that?"

"That," I said, pointing my own light at it, "is the magical tree house."

"Can I go up?"

"Yeah, just be careful. I don't know how good those steps are. Go slow!"

"Do you think—" Jenn said.

"He'll be fine," I said, although I had no idea if he would be or not.

He took each wood step one at a time but moved quickly. Soon, he disappeared into the hole in the bottom of the floor.

Then his head stuck out the hole, and he waved. We waved back.

"Is there a candle up there?" I asked.

"I don't know. It's really dark."

I handed Em over to Jenn. My wife looked at me like she didn't think this was a good idea.

I stuck the flashlight into my back pocket and carefully tested the first plank. It seemed quite sturdy, so I went up. I made it to the top and stuck my head through the hole.

"Hi!" Sam said.

"Hi!" I climbed onto the floor, pulled the flashlight out, and scanned the room. "This is a lot smaller than I remember."

"It's so cool! Look!" He pointed at the stained-glass window.

I pointed the beam at the small shelf and found the candle. There was a matchbox there. I doubted the matches inside would be any good, but it was worth a try...and it worked, first try.

I put the flame to the candle, and it caught.

It wasn't terribly bright, but it was working.

I pointed my flashlight at the window, and it highlighted the colors of the window. Soon, the little room began to glow.

"Dustin?" Jenn said from below. "You...you should come down here."

I stuck my head out the floor. "Why? Is there any—" And then I saw it. Or rather, them.

I stuck my feet out and began heading back down the ladder.

"Come on down, Sam."

A few seconds later, I was on the ground as Sam started down.

I turned and stepped up next to my wife and daughter.

The whole area was bathed in a purple fog that was both eerie and soothing.

Up ahead, in the open field, stood a deer, watching us.

Emily pointed at it but didn't say anything.

Then, coming out of the fog, was the outline of a man.

I recognized Dad immediately.

His hand reached out and stroked the deer. Then his head turned and looked at us.

I held my hand up.

He returned the gesture and smiled.

"Who's that?" Sam asked.

"That is your grandfather."

Sam looked up at me, confused.

I nodded and smiled.

Sam took a hesitant step forward, then checked with me again.

I nodded again.

He took another few steps, walking slowly forward.

The purple glow seemed to both intensify and become more dense.

Sam began to disappear into the mist, though I could still see him.

The image of my father knelt down and held out his arms.

Still doubtful, Sam moved closer until he was within arm's reach. My son looked back at me, an expression of awe on his face, something I felt throughout my body.

Sam took the last step, and Dad wrapped his arms around his grandson.

Dad's eyes looked at me, and he smiled.

I love you.

This was heard in my head.

A great warmth came over me as the light intensified even more, the figures—my dad, my son, and the deer— seeming to glow from the inside out.

It became blinding for several seconds, forcing me to hold my hand up to shield my eyes.

And then it faded somewhat to show...more figures.

I began to realize I knew them all...Mr. Wendorf, who was scowling... and yet somehow smiling; Mr. Kraus, wearing his worn baseball cap; Mrs. Kraus, who stood without her walker; Rachel, holding her briefcase with a slight smile; Robert Schultz, the school bully; Rusty, the boy who had committed suicide; even Officer Sanders, who had been found dead.

The last figure I saw was...unbelievable.

Emma stood, hands on her hips, eyes twinkling.

Oh, no, Emma! I wasn't able to say goodbye.

Then I felt a hand tug on mine. I looked down to see Sam beaming up at me. His other hand held onto the ghost of my father, who looked me in the eyes. They sparkled with delight.

His arms opened wide, and I did the same, falling into a hug that was all-embracing and loving.

I love you.

And when I opened my eyes...it was all gone.

Jenn looked at me, eyes wide and filled with tears. I felt my own slide down my cheeks. We stood there in the darkness, feeling the lingering warmth. And a loving peace came over me.

Eventually, we went back to the car, reluctantly.

Jenn leaned her head on my shoulder

"That was the most beautiful thing," she said.

I looked out into the field again.

I might have imagined it, but I swear I saw the shadowy outlines of the figures disappearing into the woods.

"Yes," I said. "The most beautiful thing."

The Legendary Story of
Holytail The Squirrel

A Bonus Story Written by Leinad Platz

Like most squirrels, he was born in the tight, cavernous quarters of an oak tree. He was one of four babies his mother gave birth to on a sun-filled spring morning.

The woods where their home was located were in the Appalachians, just outside of the quaint little town of Portsmouth in southern Ohio—nestled in the hills along the northern banks of the Ohio River in the obviously named Ohio River Valley.

From way high up in the tree where he was born, he could see far off in the distance, where a bridge stretched over the mighty river connecting Ohio to Kentucky.

While growing up, crawling in and out of the hole in the tree, his loving mother taught him and his siblings how to jump tree branch to tree branch. Then, in the fall, how to properly bury acorns that had fallen all around under the tree, storing them to eat during the upcoming long, cold winter.

Grown up, living on his own and being young and restless, he worked hard all day long to bury as many acorns as possible to prepare for winter.

A chill had set into the night, and the fall wind began to blow the leaves, full of color, off the branches, floating onto the ground, eventually turning the trees bare.

He remembered being taught by his mother and his uncle to closely listen to the drying leaves as they became "crunchy" and made noise—a sound to alarm him to potential danger. Especially hunters.

He would pop his head up and down while working hard, gathering acorns while looking and listening for hunters.

Crunch...crunch.

He quickly put his ears up as the sound grew louder. His heartbeat increasing, he darted up the tree before stopping to catch his breath and hide behind a barren branch.

Then, beneath him...the crunching stopped!

He slowly took a peek around the branch...only to see two hunters looking up.

One of the hunters spotted him and raised his gun, pointing its barrel straight at him, taking aim. He shut his eyes to pray the branch would protect him as he was caught frozen behind the branch.

Then "BANG!"...

...the gun went off...

...its bullet hitting him in the tail...

...spinning him around the branch.

Clinging on for dear life, he managed to pull himself up and scurry into the hole he called home.

His tail stung with enormous pain while he prayed, begging for the hunters to go away.

Then...

CRUNCH...CRUNCH...

The crunching faded away...

Riddled with fear, he laid shaking, recalling the time his uncle told him about the importance of hiding from the hunters because, "You don't want to become squirrel gravy over biscuits."

Time passed. He licked and licked his aching tail...until one day, it finally healed.

But once healed, he could see a perfectly round hole straight through the middle of it.

After many dark days alone, he exited from the comfort of his little home, through the hole in the side of the tree...to the sound of applauding squirrels and singing birds.

He was surprised.

He crawled out to the branch where the incident occurred and noticed the branch was scarred from where the bullet had grazed it, sparing his life.

With the memory of the incident still firmly embedded in his mind, a lump formed in his throat, and a shiver passed through him, realizing he narrowly escaped becoming "squirrel gravy over biscuits."

Embarrassed, he hid his tail so as not to show the others.

But slowly, gaining his confidence, he took a moment to stretch it out.

The clapping from the others suddenly stopped, their faces expressing surprise. There came sounds of "Oh!"

And every squirrel and bird and animal noticed his beautiful tail with a hole through the center of it.

One of the wide-eyed squirrels off in the distance shouted: "It's a third-degree miracle!"

And another staring in amazement said: "Holytail!"

And that's the story of how the legendary "Holytail The Squirrel" got his name.

The End

OTHER TITLES BY LEINAD PLATZ

Today's Most Gripping Storyteller

Sir Coffin Graves - Book 1

Sir Coffin Graves - Book 2

Visit - LeinadPlatz.com